College Life 101

CAMERON: The Sorority

COLLEGE LIFE 101

Cameron: The Sorority
Zara: The Roommate
Kim: The Party
Bridget: The Fling
Allison: The Townie
The Reunion

College Life 101

CAMERON: The Sorority

Wendy Corsi Staub

BERKLEY JAM BOOKS, NEW YORK

If you purchased this book without a cover, you should be aware that this book is stolen property. It was reported as "unsold and destroyed" to the publisher, and neither the author nor the publisher has received any payment for this "stripped book."

This is a work of fiction. Names, characters, places, and incidents either are the product of the author's imagination or are used fictitiously, and any resemblance to actual persons, living or dead, business establishments, events, or locales is entirely coincidental.

COLLEGE LIFE 101
CAMERON: THE SORORITY

A Berkley Jam Book / published by arrangement with
the author

PRINTING HISTORY
Berkley edition / November 1997
Berkley Jam edition / May 2004

Copyright © 1997 by The Berkley Publishing Group.
Cover design by Rita Frangie.

All rights reserved.
This book, or parts thereof, may not be reproduced in any form without permission. The scanning, uploading, and distribution of this book via the Internet or via any other means without the permission of the publisher is illegal and punishable by law. Please purchase only authorized electronic editions, and do not participate in or encourage electronic piracy of copyrighted materials. Your support of the author's rights is appreciated.
For information address: The Berkley Publishing Group,
a division of Penguin Group (USA) Inc.,
375 Hudson Street, New York, New York 10014.

ISBN: 0-425-19727-1

BERKLEY JAM BOOKS®
Berkley Jam Books are published by The Berkley Publishing Group,
a division of Penguin Group (USA) Inc.,
375 Hudson Street, New York, New York 10014.
BERKLEY JAM and its logo are trademarks
belonging to Penguin Group (USA) Inc.

PRINTED IN THE UNITED STATES OF AMERICA

10 9 8 7 6 5 4 3 2

For the Florida gang:
Aunt Rita, Paul Joseph, Suzanne,
Kristin, Gregg, and Andrew

And for Mark and Morgan, with love

With special thanks to Julie Bochstiegel
for filling me in on the sorority scene!

Hi, Cameron-

Where to begin? It's been a great four years—no, actually, it's been a great <u>thirteen</u> years, but I'm not going to go back to kindergarten at this point...though I will say that I've forgiven you for breaking my burnt sienna crayon in half when I wouldn't share with you. You brat! I guess we're going to miss old W.B.H.S., huh? Especially sixth-period study hall—wasn't it fun bugging Zara? That's what she gets for actually trying to study in there. Always remember those freezing cold nights at ski club—and Kim's flask of cinnamon schnapps. And when we stole the clapper from Ms. Handelman's stupid bell—I'll never forget the look on her face when she went to ring it that day. You're going to have an excellent time at South Florida—you're so lucky! Good luck, and don't forget about me, stuck back at home, going to State...(<u>sigh</u>).

XXX OOO
Allison

Hey, Cammie!

Can you believe these yearbooks _finally_ showed up? I mean, it's only _August_! Great pic of you on page 172 with the cheerleaders—that moo Kelly Douglas looks like she's totally crushing your back in the mount, yet there's the cool-under-pressure co-captain Cameron Collier, giving a peppy smile as always. Senior year was excellent, just as I predicted, right? Always remember Saturday night kegs at the Pines, cutting gym, the class trip to NYC—what a blast that was! Remember sneaking into that gross porn movie and meeting that sicko in the plaid pants? I thought you were going to pass out after he said that to you! And remember how the bus almost left without us the last day? Ms. Samanski was such a bitch about it. I always knew she hated me! Anyway, I could go on and on about all the wild times, but I won't cuz I know you can't possibly forget any of them. Have a great time in Florida—how can you not? Make sure that you save some of those buffed blond surfer dudes for me, because I'll be making a road trip A.S.A.P.—I hear midwestern winters are just as bad as here in western New York. Can you believe it? If I get frostbite one too many times, I'll transfer to south Florida—wouldn't that be a riot?

Your bud,
Kim

Cameron,

Thank God these yearbooks came in before you leave tomorrow! I can't believe you're going so early, but I know how important rushing is to you. I hope you get into the sorority of your choice—don't worry, you will. It's hard to believe that for the next four years, you and I will be as far away from each other as we can possibly get, with you in south Florida and me in Seattle. But we'll write and call, and we'll see each other in a few months for Christmas, right? That'll be fun—especially if you have one of your famous New Year's Eve parties! Thanks for everything over the past year, Cam—especially for always listening when Grant and I had our little spats. You always knew what I needed to hear. Grant says you're very wise for your years—isn't that such a Grant thing to say? I can't believe I'm going to be all alone at school—I never dreamed he wouldn't be coming with me. If you get lonely in Florida, call me, 'cuz you know I'll be lonely, too. Have fun, be good, keep smiling, and remember I love ya.

Bridget

Dear Cameron,

  First of all, let me apologize for these yearbooks being so late, since I know I'm never going to hear the end of it from everyone. I knew I shouldn't have accepted the editor-in-chief position! But like I said, it's not <u>all</u> my fault that we didn't get the stuff to the printer's on time. Thanks for all your help with the book, though—you took some excellent candids. I love the one of Allison and Kim in the cafeteria—did you see how great it looks in the layout? Page 68. Anyway, you've been a good friend, and I've enjoyed getting to know you better these past few years that we've been on the newspaper and yearbook staffs together. I hope all your dreams will come true, and that you'll keep in touch. If you need long-distance help with math this year, give me a call!

                                      Love,
                                      Zara

Chapter 1

Cameron Collier finished signing Allison DeMitri's yearbook, set it on the polished cherry end table, and glanced around at her four best friends, all of whom were still busy writing.

It was hard to believe that this was the last time the five of them would be together before...

Well, before life changed forever.

Tomorrow morning Cameron would board a jet for Fort Lauderdale, where she would begin her freshman year at South Florida State College. She'd been looking forward to it for months, ever since she'd been accepted—but now that it was almost time to go, her stomach was jumping all over the place, and not entirely from happy anticipation.

All of a sudden she was scared.

Not scared. Terrified.

She toyed with the cap of her blue ballpoint pen and stared absently out the family room window at her sister Paige's wooden swing set.

Don't be such a baby, she told herself. *You've started over plenty of times. You felt exactly the same way before you went to middle school and high school.*

But that was different.

She'd never been going off to a new experience *alone*, hundreds of miles from Weston Bay. She'd always had her friends with her.

What was she going to do without Kim Garfield and Bridget Mundy, Allison DeMitri, and Zara Benjamin? They'd been in school together since they were five years old. She still remembered meeting them the first day of kindergarten.

Zara, of course, had looked exactly the same as she did now, with horn-rimmed glasses, her dark hair in a single braid, and a perpetually intense expression in her dark brown eyes. When Miss Barnes had asked if anyone in the class knew how to read yet, she had been the only one to raise her hand.

Allison, Cameron recalled, had been really chubby back then, and she'd cried—loudly—when her mother left. Cameron remembered wondering why she was so upset. Her own parents had told her how much fun she was going to have in school, and she'd been excited about all the new toys and books in the play area, and about all the new kids to play with.

Only when Allison cried had Cameron felt a moment's hesitation... but she got over it fast. And so did Allison, thanks to Kim.

Kim, who had grown up next door to the DeMitris, had held Allison's hand all through that first day, as if protecting her. They were such opposites—Allison with her ironed satin hair ribbons and crisp new dress, and Kim in worn jeans, her blond pigtails parted crookedly and traces of a milk mustache on her freckled face. But they were friends, and whenever anyone picked on Allison, who was prone to clumsiness and to throwing up after lunch, Kim was there to defend her.

Then there was Bridget, whose sunny personality had beamed through even back then. She was tinier than any of the other five-year-olds, and her hair had been more of an orangey-red in those days, and her mother had obviously tried to tame the natural tangle of curls. She had been the maternal one who held them all together, who made sure everyone was all right. She still did.

So long ago...

And now it was time to say goodbye.

Cameron swallowed hard, thinking about how hard it had been to see her father leave last night. He'd left for a business trip to New York, where he was going to attend a seminar for African-American doctors. He'd cried when he left, hugging her so tightly against his broad chest that Cameron could barely breathe.

"Be careful down there, baby," he'd said, stroking her

smooth dark hair. "Have fun, but be careful. I mean it. And if you need anything, you call us."

"I will, Dad," she'd said, trying not to cry herself. But it hadn't worked. When she saw the tears running down her father's dark cheeks, she'd found herself sobbing as well. She'd watched him through the window as he got into his prized champagne-colored Mercedes and drove off down the winding street, watching until she could no longer see his car.

And that was the first time she'd realized how much her world was going to change within the next twenty-four hours.

Cameron turned away from the window as Kim slapped the yearbook closed abruptly, tossed it to Bridget, and said, "Done. God, my hand is killing me from all this writing."

She waved her wrist as if trying to get the kinks out, her woven purple bracelet sliding down her forearm. Her long, straight blond hair was slightly tousled, as always—she rarely bothered with a brush. She was wearing Tevas and a pair of short, faded denim cutoffs with a tie-dyed T-shirt that was casually knotted above her flat abdomen.

"You'd better get used to writing, Kim," Bridget said. "I expect a lot of letters from all of you this year."

"I never write letters," Kim told her, getting up restlessly and wandering over to the sliding glass doors that led to the Colliers' redwood deck. "I'll call instead."

"No, you won't," Allison said. She, like the others, was dressed more conservatively than Kim, wearing plain khaki shorts and a short-sleeved polo shirt. "You're terrible about keeping in touch. Last summer when you went to Camp Timberview, I heard from you exactly once."

"I didn't hear from you at all," Cameron said.

"Well, you weren't around most of the summer, anyway," Kim pointed out, pulling a pack of cigarettes out of her back pocket and opening the sliding glass door. "You were on the Colliers' excellent adventure, remember?"

That was what her friends had dubbed the four-week trip to Europe Cameron had taken with her mother and younger sisters a year ago. Shelley Collier, a freelance photographer, had landed an important assignment for a travel magazine and had decided to take her daughters along. It had been a whirlwind—London, Paris, Brussels, Venice, Madrid. Cameron's father, a pediatrician, had joined them for the final two weeks in August, and they'd spent them in the south of France, basking in the sun on the Mediterranean. It was pure heaven.

She'd even met a guy there, Jean-Louis. He'd thought she was much older, of course—she hadn't dared tell him she'd just turned seventeen, since he was in his mid-twenties.

"Hey, Cam, have you heard from that French guy lately?" Bridget asked, as if reading her mind.

"Not since Christmas." She shrugged, remembering how she'd been determined to keep in touch with Jean-Louis when they'd said goodbye last summer. Then school had begun, and she'd started dating Derek Mesner, a cute football player from Weston Bay's rival team. She'd forgotten all about Jean-Louis....

Then she'd forgotten Derek when she'd hooked up with Kent Quimby, a sophomore at the state university only fifteen miles from Weston Bay....

"I wonder what the guys in Florida are going to be like," she mused, the jitters in her stomach becoming less fear-inspired and more anticipatory once again. She went over to close the sliding glass door behind Kim, who had stepped out onto the deck to smoke.

Zara rolled her eyes. "Ever hear the word *himbo*?"

"That's not fair," Allison said. "Just because they'll be incredibly great-looking with amazing bodies doesn't mean they'll be stupid!"

"Relax, I was only kidding." Zara flashed a rare teasing grin. "I'm just jealous."

"Well, nobody told you to go to a women's college," Bridget pointed out. "I don't know how you're going to live without guys for four years."

"My mother said it was fine," Zara said, though her brown eyes betrayed her own slight misgivings. "She said the coed parties were really fun, and that the Dannon campus was crawling with Ivy League men every weekend. You really appreciate guys when you don't see them on a daily basis. And she said it was better to live among women—it was a very nurturing, supportive environment."

"Yeah, but your mother went to Dannon, when? Twenty years ago?" Bridget asked. "I bet things are way different now. Back then it was more normal to go to a school that wasn't coed."

CAMERON: THE SORORITY

"I'm sure it'll be fine," Cameron said quickly, feeling sorry for Zara.

They all knew that she'd only chosen to attend ultracompetitive Dannon College because it was her mother's alma mater. The Benjamins, both professors, had always pressured their daughter to follow a certain path.

And Zara had obediently followed it. Throughout their years at Weston Bay, she'd devoted more time to studying than anything else. She was valedictorian of their senior class, had won numerous scholarships, and had chosen a pre-med program for college, even though Cameron privately wondered if her heart was really in it.

"Anyway," Cameron added, wanting to banish the uncertainty from Zara's face, "I'm going to be living in a sorority house with only women, too. *If* I get asked to pledge."

"You will," Bridget assured her.

"You *better*," Allison said. "After leaving so early for school and everything. You're going to miss Kim's pre-Labor Day party at the Pines."

"I know, but I can't help it. Rushing starts two weeks before classes."

"That sorority stuff is pretty intense in the South, huh?" Allison commented. "Are you sure you want to do something like that?"

"Positive," Cameron said. She'd known, ever since she'd visited the South Florida State campus, that she wanted to join a sorority. That way she'd get to live in one of the stately old mansions on Sorority Row. She'd be surrounded by close, caring friends, just as she always had been here in Weston Bay. And there'd be parties, and dances, and big football weekends...

She could hardly wait.

Kim poked her head back in, a burning cigarette in her hand.

Cameron made a face at it. Her friend's smoking habit was a bone of contention among the others. But Kim did as she pleased; she always had, paying no heed to advice—or, sometimes, to rules... or laws.

"It's sweltering out here, Cam," she said plaintively, swiping at a trickle of sweat on her forehead. "It must be a hundred degrees. Are you sure I can't smoke inside?"

"No way. You know my mother would kill me. I've told you a million times she doesn't allow smoking in the house."

Cameron's mother had grown up in Georgia, where, according to her, everyone had smoked—including her own parents. Cameron's grandfather, Reece Bainbridge, had died of lung cancer just last year.

Cameron still vividly remembered the argument her mother had had with her grandmother at the wake, over the fact that her grandmother was still chain-smoking.

"How can you do that when you know it killed Daddy?" her mother had demanded when she'd caught Myra Bainbridge lighting up on the steps of the funeral home.

"This isn't what killed your father, and you know it," her grandmother had shot back, inhaling deeply.

CAMERON: THE SORORITY

Cameron had wondered what that was supposed to mean, and she didn't understand her mother's next comment, either.

"It's been twenty years, Mother," Shelly had said wearily, running a hand through her short blond hair. "You know Daddy died of cancer. Those damn cigarettes destroyed his lungs."

Her grandmother's glaring silence and pursed lips had left a lasting impression on Cameron.

She'd wondered, occasionally, in the months since, why the Colliers had never been close to her mother's side of the family. Granted, they lived hundreds of miles away—but it wasn't as if Cameron's parents didn't like to travel. They were always jetting off somewhere, and when Cameron was younger, they'd often driven to New York City to visit her father's side of the family. It seemed they just didn't like to go to Georgia—or, since her grandparents had moved to a retirement community in Boca Raton, to Florida.

Cameron's decision to go to college in Fort Lauderdale had nothing to do with the fact that her grandmother was living only a few hours from campus. After all, she'd seen the woman only about a dozen times in her life—unlike her father's mother.

Elma Collier had moved in with them back when Cameron was in middle school, after Grandpa Eddie had died of a heart attack back in Brooklyn. She'd lived with the Colliers until two years ago, when they'd had to put her into a nursing home after she fell and broke her hip. Now they visited her every weekend, and she was still spry as ever.

Yesterday, when Cameron had gone over to say goodbye, Grandma Elma had given her a crisp hundred-dollar bill and told her to buy something nice to wear at her first college dance.

She was so different from Myra Bainbridge, Cameron thought. Her mother's mother had sent her a card and a sizable check in response to the graduation announcement Cameron had mailed her back in June. But there had been no warm words or well wishes in the card, and no mention of the fact that her grandmother wouldn't be flying up north for the ceremony or for Cameron's party the following weekend.

Grandma Elma had been there, though, beaming from her wheelchair in the front row when Cameron, who was class secretary, had led everyone in the Pledge of Allegiance.

"Hey, Cam?" Bridget cut into her thoughts. "Mind if I use the phone to call Grant? He's supposed to be getting off work at four, and I'm going to tell him to pick me up here instead of at home."

"No problem." Cameron watched as her friend walked up the three steps leading to the large, sunny kitchen. She wondered what it would be like to be Bridget, so in love and so sure of herself though she was only seventeen. Bridget never seemed to have a doubt about her relationship with Grant, whom she had been dating since they were sophomores. In fact, she went about everything in her life with a capable, confident air that Cameron envied.

"Hey, did you guys get thank-you notes from Grant?" Allison whispered as soon as Bridget was out of earshot.

"I did," Cameron said, thinking of the short, awkward note Bridget's boyfriend had penned, expressing his and his mother's gratitude for the flowers she'd sent to the funeral home and the cake she'd brought over when his father had died in June.

"Me, too," Zara said. "How's he doing? Does anyone know?"

"Not that great," Allison commented. "It was such a shock—I mean, I still can't believe it. Mr. Caddaham was so young, and he seemed like he was in such great shape. He always went jogging by our house every morning, rain or shine. Who would expect someone like that to drop dead of a heart attack? He was barely forty years old!"

"I know, but Bridget said they found out there was a history of heart disease in their family," Cameron remembered. "I guess Grant had some great-uncle who died when he was, like, twenty-nine."

Allison shuddered. "Can you imagine that?"

"I'm thinking of becoming a cardiologist," Zara said in her quiet way. "Ever since that happened to Mr. Caddaham, I've been thinking it would be a good idea."

"That's great, Zara," Allison told her. "But don't you think it would be tough?"

"What do you mean?"

"You know...always having to deal with people's health problems. Having to tell them bad news—that would be so hard."

"It *would* be hard, but rewarding, too," Cameron pointed out, wrapping a strand of her long, thick black hair around her finger. "I mean, look at my dad. He gets the satisfaction of knowing he's helping all those sick little kids."

"Yeah, he was great with me when I had mono last year," Zara said. "I hope my bedside manner is that warm."

"It will be," Allison assured her.

"Well, that's the least of my worries, actually. First I have to get through four years of pre-med—"

"*Without* men," Kim interjected, stepping back inside just in time to hear the conversation.

"Without men," Zara agreed. "Which is probably better, anyway. I won't have all that distraction, so I'll be able to concentrate on studying."

"Well, if you find you can't live without *distraction*, you can always transfer to Summervale and move in with me," Kim said blithely, flopping down on the overstuffed green brocade couch.

"Or you can come to Florida," Cameron told Zara, keeping a vigilant eye on Kim, whose legs were dangling in perilous proximity to a framed prizewinning photo her mother had taken.

"Florida? I don't think so."

"Why not?" Surprised, Cameron glanced at Zara and saw that she was wrinkling her nose in distaste.

"Let me guess." Allison held up a forefinger. "Your parents don't think southerners take education seriously enough."

CAMERON: THE SORORITY

"It's not that." Zara looked uncomfortable, and Cameron realized Allison's words were partly true. The Benjamins wouldn't approve of a school like South Florida State, which was more famous for its annual MTV-televised beach volleyball tournament than it was for its academic program.

Not that she cared—she was going to college mainly to have fun, not to hole up for four years in some fiercely competitive environment.

"Then what's wrong?" Kim asked Zara, propping her elbow on a pillow and her chin in her hand. "Are there too many boys down in Florida to distract you with their tanned, sculpted chests and bulging biceps?"

Zara smiled faintly. "There probably are, but...well, you know. The Ku Klux Klan..." She trailed off.

"The *Ku Klux Klan?*" Cameron echoed. "What about them?"

"They don't like Jews, that's what. When my dad gave a lecture down in Mississippi a few years ago, he got hassled. There's a lot of that in the South. I'm surprised you want to go there, Cameron."

Kim laughed. "You think a bunch of torch-carrying losers in pillowcases are going to go after Cameron because her dad's black? Come on, Zara. That's crazy."

"Besides, Cameron looks white, so it's not like anyone will even know," Allison said, then winced and added, "I didn't mean anything bad by that, Cam, I just—"

"I know you didn't," Cameron interrupted, suddenly feeling uncomfortable—and irritated by the turn the conversation had taken. The subject of her mixed-race background had never been an issue among her friends.

In fact, for a small town, Weston Bay was remarkably liberal and diverse, and the Colliers generally hadn't had to deal with racism. There was only once, when Cameron was really little, that she'd been confronted in an ugly playground incident. Jamie Reynolds, the third-grade bully, had sidled up to her and demanded, "How come your mom married a nigger?"

Cameron remembered staring at him, bewildered. Then Kim, who was with her, had dropped her end of the jump rope and socked Jamie in the stomach, which had shut him up until his family moved away the following summer.

That was it. Just that one episode.

Oh, there had been times, when the Colliers were at the mall in Buffalo, or traveling, when her parents had been on the receiving end of strangers' curious or even hostile stares. But that had never really bothered Cameron, and her parents seemed to shrug it off.

Now she wondered if Zara was right about going to school down South. What if the Ku Klux Klan *did* come after her? The idea seemed preposterous, but it wasn't as though Cameron was naive enough to think racism didn't exist outside her own safe, familiar little world.

The butterflies in her stomach became hyperactive hummingbirds, and she was relieved when Bridget reappeared and everyone dropped the Klan conversation.

"Grant already left," she said, looking concerned. "I tried

CAMERON: THE SORORITY

him at home, but his mother said he's not there yet. So I'm going to get going if no one minds—he's probably on his way to my house."

"I'll come, too," Zara said, standing and picking up her yearbook.

"Are you sure?" Cameron asked. "I can drive you home later."

"No, it's okay, I'll ride back with Bridget. My brother's home this week, and I want to spend some time with him before he goes back to Brown."

Cameron nodded. Zara and her older brother, Aaron, were extremely close. Her friend's chatter was invariably sprinkled with "Aaron says..." or "Guess what Aaron did?" She knew that Zara had chosen to attend Dannon College in part because it was located in a small Massachusetts town not far from Providence, Rhode Island, where Aaron was in his first year of medical school.

It would be nice, Cameron thought, if she knew someone else in Florida—besides her grandmother Bainbridge, that was. She didn't count, because Cameron had no intention of looking her up. But it would be nice to have someone nearby, just in case she got lonely....

"I guess we should get going, too," Allison said, glancing at Kim, who nodded.

The two of them had walked over together. Their neighborhood wasn't far from Maplebridge Heights, the development where Cameron lived, but it might as well have been a world away. The crowded houses on working-class Finch Street, where both Allison and Kim lived, were situated on postage-stamp lots, with chain-link fences and a panel truck in every other driveway.

In contrast, the Colliers' modern green-shuttered colonial was perched at the end of a quiet cul-de-sac on a landscaped, sloping lot dotted with plenty of leafy trees. There was a three-car garage in front and a built-in pool out back.

This, Cameron knew, was her parents' dream house, the one they'd imagined back when they were newlyweds and her mother was working two jobs to put her father through medical school. They'd had it built when Cameron was in fifth grade, after her father's practice became established and her mother started receiving regular magazine assignments.

The house was comfortably upscale, but not showy, and there was plenty of room for Cameron to entertain her friends—which she often did. So did her sisters, fifteen-year-old Hayley, who at the moment was splashing in the pool with a bunch of her pals, and Paige, who was eleven and currently in bed with a summer virus.

"I can't believe you guys are all leaving me," Cameron said, watching her friends gather their yearbooks and purses. "I mean, this is it. I'm going away tomorrow. We're not going to see each other for ages."

"You said yourself you have a million things to do, Cam," Bridget said, fidgeting with the engraved heart keychain Grant had given her for her birthday. "You're not even packed yet."

CAMERON: THE SORORITY

"I just have my carry-on left to do."

"And you have to go to Mailboxes, Etc., to ship your second trunk," Zara pointed out. "I can't believe you waited until now."

"Well, we're not all as organized as you are, Zara," Kim said with a grin. "Allison said you're completely packed, and you don't even leave for three weeks."

"Not *completely* packed." Zara's cheeks were tinged with red. "I just hate waiting till the last minute."

"Okay, whatever, let's go," Bridget said, jangling her keys. "I've got to track down Grant."

"Hey, wait," Cameron told Bridget. "I've got that Goo Goo Dolls CD you loaned me. It's upstairs. Just let me—"

"It's okay," Bridget said. "You can borrow it for the semester. I'm not going to have a CD player at school, anyway." Her green eyes looked somber as she reached out for Cameron. "Listen, Cam—"

"I know. Don't say it. You'll make me cry," Cameron said, swallowing over the lump that was already rising in her throat. "Just give me a hug and get out of here, okay?"

One by one her friends squeezed her shoulders, and Allison, who was last, planted a kiss on her cheek, saying, "That's for luck. I hope you get into the best sorority on campus, Cam."

"I hope so, too," she said, her voice catching as the four of them headed for the sliding glass doors. "I'm going to miss you guys. You'd better write!"

"We will," Zara called, stepping out into the hot August sun.

"Not me," Kim said over her shoulder. "But I swear I'll call. Well, maybe I'll write, too. You never know. I might be incredibly bored at college."

"You?" Allison hooted at that. "Can you guys imagine that? That's like Zara saying she might not feel like studying at college."

"Or like Cameron deciding she doesn't feel like rushing after all," Bridget put in.

"Or like you breaking up with Grant," Cameron called, not to be outdone.

"Never in a million years," Bridget said, waving her heart-shaped key chain and tossing her auburn curls.

It wasn't until they were gone—the friends with whom Cameron had shared most of her days—and she was left all alone that the tears started trickling down her cheeks.

Chapter 2

Only when the plane lifted off from the Buffalo airport, leaving suburban Cheektowaga far below, did Cameron lean back in her seat and breath a sigh of relief.

It had been a harrowing morning. Her mother, who was supposed to drive her to the airport, had been up with Paige all night. She'd had to run to the pharmacy to pick up a prescription for her first thing this morning and had been late getting back. By the time she pulled into the driveway, Cameron had been in a panic. She'd barely taken the time to hug Hayley and Paige and snatch her carry-on bag off the floor before dashing out to the car.

The trip to the airport normally took forty-five minutes, but at that hour the thruway had been clogged with Buffalo's rush-hour traffic. By the time they got there, Cameron's flight was already boarding. She'd been forced to give her mother a quick hug and kiss and dash to the gate.

It was probably better that way, she decided as she leaned back in her seat and adjusted the air-flow valve overhead. At least her mother hadn't had time to get into a heavy-duty goodbye scene. Neither of them had even cried, although her mother's voice had sounded suspiciously high-pitched, and Cameron's eyes had been stinging as she headed down the jetway.

But all that was behind her now. She was on her way.

She smoothed her navy silk pants, thinking that she was going to be a wrinkled mess by the time she got off the plane in Lauderdale. She probably should have worn jeans, or even shorts. But she'd wanted to dress up for the occasion, thinking that it was one of the most important days of her life.

So she'd worn the new silk pants with a boxy ivory blazer, and she'd piled her long, thick dark hair on top of her head in an elaborate twist that had taken twenty minutes and a major pile of bobby pins to create. She had also taken the time to accent her large, dark eyes with smudgy black liner and plenty of mascara, and her full mouth with her new mulberry-colored lipstick. She hadn't bothered with facial foundation or blusher, though. She rarely did. Her complexion was naturally dark-toned, and her cheeks were still rosy from spending the previous weekend outside at her parents' country club pool, where she'd been life-guarding all summer. She had a deep, even tan all over.

CAMERON: THE SORORITY 25

She had been aware of several men turning their heads to look at her as she hurried toward Gate Five in the airport, and she'd been glad she'd taken the time to get fixed up. She knew she was a naturally attractive girl, that her looks were "exotic," as her mother was always saying. But back in Weston Bay, it was easy not to bother with her hair or makeup or getting dressed up. She'd spent most of the summer bumming around in shorts, her hair braided or pulled back in a careless ponytail.

That would have to change now. She wouldn't get asked to pledge a sorority if she looked like a slob.

She checked her watch and shifted restlessly in her seat, wishing someone were sitting next to her. But apparently, there weren't many people interested in flying to Fort Lauderdale in the middle of August, and the entire row was empty.

Cameron wished she'd brought something to read. There hadn't even been time to buy a magazine or a newspaper in the airport newsstand. And she'd planned to bring her yearbook, which she'd barely had a chance to glance at yet, but it would have made her carry-on bag way too heavy. Instead, she'd been forced to tuck it into her remaining trunk, which meant she wouldn't be seeing it again for almost a week.

Well, a few more days wouldn't make much difference— she'd been waiting to see the yearbook all summer long. As one of the student photographers, she was responsible for most of the candids, and she was anxious to see how they'd reproduced. She knew she'd taken some pretty good shots.

Her mother had been so excited when she'd discovered

that Cameron was interested in photography. It wasn't like she wanted to follow in Shelley Collier's footsteps and become a pro, or anything, but it would be fun to take pictures as a hobby, Cameron figured.

When it came to careers, she had no idea what she wanted to do. But it was no big deal. She had plenty of time to decide. And at least she knew what she *didn't* want to do—anything that would mean slaving away at her studies for the next ten years of her life, the way her father had in med school and the way Zara would have to.

Cameron liked school, but primarily for social reasons. She was fortunate enough to be naturally bright, so that she hadn't had to work very hard to keep her grades up at Weston Bay High. Her father was always telling her she was an underachiever, and that with her IQ, she should be at the top of her class. But in Cameron's opinion, it wouldn't have been worth it.

Look at Zara. She'd studied constantly and graduated at the top of their class, and where had it gotten her? Facing four years at a women's college, taking pre-med courses like anatomy and biology. She'd be lucky if she had time to do her laundry.

Cameron, on the other hand, was planning to keep her course load as light as possible for the first semester. She didn't want anything to interfere with pledging, which was sure to take up a lot of her time.

She closed her eyes and pictured the excitement that lay

ahead. These first two weeks would be filled with parties and teas and informal get-togethers sponsored by different sororities, who would evaluate the freshmen hopefuls and decide which ones were serious pledge candidates. For the second round of gatherings, the sororities would only invite back the girls they were seriously considering.

What if you're not one of them? Cameron asked herself. *Or what if only the geeky sororities want you?*

She wasn't sure there even were geeky sororities at South Florida, but it seemed likely. And if they were the only ones who wanted her, she'd die.

In fact, she'd rather not pledge at all, if she couldn't pledge one of the good sororities.

And if she didn't pledge...

Well, she'd rather not go to college at all if she couldn't join a sorority.

Come on, Cameron. Aren't you being a little extreme? she asked herself, then decided that she wasn't.

She knew that she was destined to live in one of those graceful houses on sorority row, to wear a gleaming pledge pin on her clothes, to join hands with a group of loyal sisters and sing corny songs...

"Can I offer you something to drink?"

The flight attendant's voice interrupted Cameron's reverie. She blinked and said, "Uh, sure. I'll have... coffee."

Not that she ever drank it at home. On the few occasions she'd taken a sip from her mother's always-full-and-steaming mug, she'd found it unpleasantly bitter. But now that she was an adult, out on her own, it was time to give it another try. After all, everyone knew that college students drank a lot of coffee.

And it wasn't so bad, Cameron decided as the plane winged its way down the East Coast and she sipped her hot drink. In fact, it was actually pretty good. All you had to do was add two sugars and three creamers.

The first thing Cameron saw, when she stepped out of the cab in front of McMahon Hall, was the blonde in the bright coral-colored bikini.

She was hard to miss, the way she was sprawled out on the lawn listening to a nearby boom box, her long, lean limbs all oil-slicked as if she were at the beach.

Cameron wasn't the only one who'd noticed her. The cab-driver had a hard time focusing on getting her carry-on bag out of the trunk, and when she tipped him five dollars—a very generous tip, considering it had been a fifteen-minute trip and he'd only had to help her with one measly bag—he'd barely said thanks.

The blonde sat up as Cameron made her way toward the front entrance of the dorm, shading her eyes with her hand. "Hi," she called, waving. "I'm Lisa Bettencourt. Y'all sure have a great tan."

Cameron was a little taken aback at the overt greeting, and

decided it was true what her mother always said about southerners being really friendly. This girl's drawl was more pronounced than Scarlett O'Hara's, and she was wearing a warm grin.

"Thanks. I'm Cameron Collier," she said, stopping a few feet from the blonde and setting down her bag for a moment. The thing weighed a ton. Good thing she hadn't crammed the yearbook in, too.

"Are y'all here early to rush?"

It took a second for Cameron to decipher the girl's accent, and when she did, she nodded. "What about you?"

"Yep. I'm so glad to see someone else. This place is empty." She waved a hand at the nondescript concrete building behind them, which did look deserted.

"Where is everyone?" Cameron asked.

"I guess they'll be arriving later today. I came two days ago. I wanted to get settled in and all, so I could concentrate on Rush Week. I wanted to work on my tan, too, so I'd look my best at the parties."

Cameron nodded, thinking this girl was taking the sorority business pretty seriously. "Where are you from?" she asked.

"Mobile, Alabama," the girl said proudly. "My family was one of the town's founders way back when. How about you?"

"I'm from New York."

The girl looked impressed. "I've always wanted to go there. Do you live near Saks Fifth Avenue?"

"Oh...not that New York. I meant the state. I'm from the

Buffalo area, actually... Weston Bay?" she added futilely, not expecting the girl to recognize it.

She didn't, because she simply looked blank and said, "I've heard it snows so much in Buffalo that sometimes they shut down the malls and everything. Why would y'all want to live up there?"

Cameron bristled. "I love it there," she said defensively. "I love snow."

Which wasn't exactly the truth. Part of the reason she'd decided to come South for college was because she'd had it with cold, snowy winters. She was tired of spending six months out of the year shivering and bundled into several layers of wool. She hated when her hands and lips cracked and bled from being chapped, and when frequent blizzards wreaked havoc on her social life.

She was psyched at the prospect of living in a place where the sun shone just about every day of the year, and the balmy ocean beaches were a hop, skip and jump away, and she could wear madras shorts in December.

But she wasn't about to admit that to Lisa Bettencourt, whose perpetual smile wasn't as warm as she'd first thought. There was no denying that the girl was gorgeous, though. She had blue eyes, high cheekbones, and one of those perfect beach bunny bodies, with a long, narrow waist, tapered thighs unmarred by cellulite, and full breasts that were spilling out of her skimpy top. Her skin was evenly browned to the delicate color of whole-wheat toast, and her long, loose hair was sun-streaked. She wore a delicate gold chain around her neck and another around her ankle, and her fingernails and toenails were polished a coral shade that exactly matched her bikini.

"How'd y'all get so tan in Buffalo?"

"It doesn't snow there in the summer," she said a little curtly.

Lisa laughed, which made Cameron feel a shade more friendly.

"Which sorority do y'all want to pledge?" she asked, and Cameron shrugged.

"I'm not sure."

"I'm planning to go with the Omega Theta Taus," Lisa informed her. "They're the *crème de la crème*."

"How do you know that?"

"Everyone knows that. Besides, my mother was an Omega," she said a bit smugly. "So I'm a legacy. But that doesn't always guarantee you'll get asked to pledge. At least, not the Omegas. They're ultra-choosy."

"Oh." Cameron wasn't sure what else to say.

"But you know, y'all should consider the Lambda Chi Kappas," Lisa said, implying that Cameron shouldn't get her hopes pinned on the Omegas. "There are quite a few northerners in it, and their house is one of the nicest ones on campus, after the Omegas', of course. It's real charming."

"Uh-huh..."

"But whatever you do, don't even glance twice at the Sigma Delta Epsilons," Lisa continued. "They'll try and suck you in, but ignore them. They're total lowlifes. And you should see their house. It totally needs a paint job, and the top step is rotting. No one in their right mind would want to live there."

"Huh." Cameron thoughtfully picked up her bag again. "Well, I'd better go get registered and find my dorm."

"I'll come along," Lisa said, promptly standing and turning off her radio before picking up the boom box and the towel she'd been lying on. "You'll be in Thayer, like me. That's the only dorm that's open this week. I can show y'all around."

"It's all right. You don't have to..."

"I want to," Lisa told her. "I've been wasting away here alone. It's great to have someone to talk to. Do y'all have a boyfriend?"

"Not at the moment," Cameron said, thinking of Skeet Thompson, the lifeguard she'd dated on and off all summer. But it wasn't anything serious. With her, it never was—especially lately.

The last thing she'd wanted to do was fall in love with someone in Weston Bay. Then she'd be in Bridget's boat, being torn about going off to college and leaving a boyfriend behind.

Not that Bridget had intended to do that in the first place. She and Grant were supposed to go to Seattle together—which Cameron had privately thought wasn't such a good idea. But then Grant's dad had passed away in June, and now Grant, an only child, couldn't just go off to the opposite side of the country and leave his mom all alone...

"I have two boyfriends," Lisa was saying as they walked up the steps to the building that housed the residency liaison offices.

She seemed to be waiting for Cameron to comment, so she dutifully echoed, "*Two* boyfriends?"

"Yup. They're both real cute. One, J.C., plays football at 'Bama. He wanted me to stay there and go to school real bad, but I didn't."

Obviously, Cameron thought as Lisa rattled on.

"The reason I didn't is that there's no Omega chapter at 'Bama. The other guy, Scotty, is better looking than J.C., but he's kind of dumb, if you know what I mean. He doesn't go to school. My mother hates him—can you get the door? My hand is all greasy from the Hawaiian Tropic."

Cameron transferred her bag to her left hand and opened the door. She stepped into a small lobby, followed by Lisa, whose bare feet made a smacking sound on the tile floor.

"Y'all need to go down the hall to the first door on the left. That's the residency office," Lisa said, pointing. "I'm going to go wash up in the ladies' room down the hall."

Cameron made her way to the room Lisa had specified and saw that the door was propped open with a chair. A bespectacled young man sat behind a desk. He glanced up from a paperback novel, stuck his finger in to mark the page, and looked at her expectantly.

"Hi," she said. "I'm Cameron Collier."

"Cameron," he said pleasantly, with no trace of a drawl. "Nice to meet you. Welcome to SFC."

She spent the next ten minutes filling out papers and waiting while the man behind the desk tried to figure out which room at Thayer she belonged in. It seemed the files were out of order because someone named Darlene, who the guy behind the desk kept cursing under his breath, hadn't done her job properly the day before.

"She can room with me," Lisa, who had reappeared, offered at one point, only to be told that the room assignments had already been made, and they couldn't go switching things around now.

Cameron was relieved at that. It wasn't that she hated Lisa, but she wasn't exactly the kind of person she wanted for a roommate. She felt a sharp pang in her chest as she thought wistfully of Bridget and Zara and Allison and Kim. Wouldn't it have been great if one of them had come to Florida with her and could be her roommate?

Then again, this dorm situation wasn't permanent. She'd be moving into a sorority house after this semester anyway.

She hoped.

"Okay, here you are," the man said at last, looking up and handing her a packet, a magnetic security card that would open the outer entrances to the dorm, and a room key. "You're on the second floor, all the way down at the end. Your roommate's name is Shanta Sahir, but she won't be here until classes start."

"*What*'s her name?" Lisa asked, leaning on the desk at Cameron's elbow.

CAMERON: THE SORORITY

He repeated it, and Lisa wrinkled her nose. "What kind of name is that?"

"I'd say it's Indian," he said, giving her a level look.

Cameron shifted her weight from her left foot to her right. "Am I all set to get into my room then?"

"You're all set," he said, smiling. "Let me know if you have any trouble."

She thanked him, then headed the short distance across campus with Lisa dogging her heels, chattering endlessly.

Thayer Hall was practically identical to Laughlin Hall, where Cameron had stayed during orientation in July. Just a big stucco box with rows of windows and a set of double glass doors in front.

"I'll show y'all how to work the card key," Lisa said, plucking it out of Cameron's hand and inserting it into a metal slot with the stripe facing down.

There was a faint clicking sound, and they were able to pull the doors open.

"We go this way," Lisa said, clearly enjoying her role as tour guide. "You'll be on the opposite end of the second floor from me. I'm in Two B. My roommate's coming from Atlanta later this afternoon. I've been e-mailing with her for the past few weeks. Have you written your roommate?"

"Not really."

"What do you mean?"

Cameron wasn't in the mood to explain that the roommate she was originally supposed to have, a girl named Karyn from

Denver, had decided not to come to Florida after all. She'd been disappointed, having spoken to her on the phone a few times and liked her.

She hadn't heard of her new roommate, Shanta, until now, but she figured that was no big deal. After all, they'd only be rooming together temporarily, since Cameron would be moving to a sorority house next semester.

She *hoped*.

Desperately... since she didn't think she could take four years of Thayer Hall.

As they walked down the long corridor, Cameron took in the battered-looking, brown-painted closed doors and the yellow cinderblock walls. The place looked less inviting than it had when she'd toured the campus last spring.

Of course then it had been filled with students. The halls had reverberated with voices and music from several different stereos, and most of the doors had been casually propped open and decorated with memo boards and posters and photos.

"Isn't this place gross?" Lisa commented, echoing Cameron's thoughts.

"It's not that bad," she lied.

"Sure it is. But it doesn't matter. It's only temporary. We'll be moving into sorority houses in no time."

"What if we don't get into a sorority?" To her own dismay, Cameron found herself echoing Lisa's chummy use of *we*.

The girl's jaw dropped open in horror. "God, don't even

CAMERON: THE SORORITY

say that. We'll get in. Even if it's not the Omegas—although if it's not, I'm doomed—I'm sure someone will ask us to pledge."

"I hope so."

"As long as it's not the Sigs."

"This is my room." Cameron stopped in front of a door marked 2S and inserted her key into the lock. "Well, thanks for everything," she told Lisa, turning around. "I guess I'll see you later."

The girl looked taken aback, as though she'd intended to barge right into the room with Cameron. "Want to get together for dinner tonight?" she asked promptly. "There's only one dining hall open, as of today, and breakfast and lunch today were awful. I have a car. We can go off campus for burgers or something."

"Actually, I want to eat in the dining hall," Cameron said, then decided she was sounding more unfriendly than she'd intended. She wanted to discourage Lisa, not make an enemy of her.

"The thing is," she expanded awkwardly, "I've been waiting my whole life to go away to college. I want to see what it's like—dining hall and all."

"Whatever." Lisa suddenly seemed aloof. "I'll see you later then."

It wasn't until she'd gone that Cameron realized she didn't even know what room Lisa was in. Not that she planned to become pals with her or anything—but suddenly, as she pushed open the door to the empty, generic dorm room, she felt very alone. More alone than she ever had in her whole life.

Luckily, the trunk Cameron's father had shipped to Florida two weeks ago was waiting in her room. It was the first thing she saw when she opened the door. The thing hadn't seemed big enough back at home—particularly when she was trying to jam it with a year's worth of stuff—but here in the dorm room, it looked enormous.

Where on earth was she going to store it—not to mention the second one, which was on the way—when she'd finished unpacking?

She glanced around the room, disheartened to see that it was a lot smaller—and more dilapidated—than the room she'd stayed in at orientation. Or maybe it was just that this room was totally bare, except for pairs of identical twin beds, dressers, and desks. But... shouldn't the stark, bare-walled emptiness make the place seem *larger*?

Back to the trunk—its presence somehow managing to be comfortably familiar yet intimidating at the same time.

What was she supposed to do with all the *crap* she'd insisted on bringing?

Suddenly feeling weary, Cameron plopped herself down on it. She remembered how excited she'd been when Grandma Elma had given it to her at graduation. The pair of steamer trunks had been wedding gifts to Grandma's parents, Great-

CAMERON: THE SORORITY

grandma Annie and Great-grandpa Sam, on their wedding day back in the nineteen teens. Grandma Elma and Grandpa Eddie had used them for their own honeymoon—they'd taken a train to Chicago—and then the two trunks had sat idly in their Brooklyn bedroom for nearly fifty years.

But Cameron's father had taken them to a restoration specialist last spring, and Grandma Elma had paid to have them lovingly relined and retooled. Now they smelled only faintly musty, and the brass detailing gleamed. Cameron had been so happy to get them...

Until now.

"What the heck am I going to do with them?" she muttered aloud.

She'd better hope that Shanta Sahir—was that her name?—was an understanding roommate...

An understanding roommate who not only didn't mind clutter, but who hadn't brought many of her own belongings to college.

With a sigh, Cameron got up, opened the lid, and started unpacking the mountain of possessions.

It was mostly clothes, along with some sheets and towels and the patchwork quilt her mother had made her back when she was into crafts a few years ago. The other trunk, the one that she'd shipped yesterday, was filled with her more personal belongings—stuffed animals and her favorite books and a bunch of photo albums and scrapbooks, not to mention her yearbook.

This one also contained last-minute things she hadn't thought she'd need. Obviously, her parents had had other ideas and had filled the trunk with a first-aid kit, countless tubes of sun protection lotion in every possible SPF, some bags of dried fruit and bottles of vitamins, and a stack of envelopes that were stamped and addressed to them. And the bulky winter coat her mother had insisted she bring, "just in case."

"Just in case what, Mom?" Cameron had asked, exasperated. "In case South Florida has an exceptionally snowy winter?"

"You never know," Shelley Collier had said, shrugging. "Don't forget, I grew up in the Deep South, Cameron. It wasn't always beach weather year-round."

"But you were way north, Mom, in *Georgia*. We're talking Fort Lauderdale here."

But Cameron had learned long ago that arguing with her mother was futile. The woman was as stubborn as they came, something her father had been saying for years.

"Once your mother makes up her mind," he would tell his daughters, "there's no changing it."

But somehow, he generally seemed to find his wife's little quirk charming, rather than infuriating.

Actually, Cameron's parents had a pretty amazing relationship. They rarely argued, and they often held hands and even kissed—a habit Cameron wasn't crazy about, particularly when they did it in front of her friends.

Not that her friends thought it was so embarrassing.

CAMERON: THE SORORITY

"I think it's cool the way your mom and dad are always so cuddly," Allison had told Cameron not long ago.

"Yeah, they get along so much better than most married people their age," added Kim, whose mother had been through two husbands—neither of whom was Kim's father, who had left her when she'd found out she was pregnant.

"And they've had to deal with so much," Allison had added.

Cameron had wondered then—and she wondered again now—what, exactly her friend had meant by that. Her parents *had* struggled during the early years, with her mother putting her father through medical school, and his always having to study—then work interminable hours during his residency. But she didn't think that was what Allison was talking about.

More likely, she meant that Cameron's mother was white and her father was black. And that, everyone assumed, must have caused problems along the way.

But as far as Cameron knew, their mixed marriage hadn't been that big a deal. Grandma Elma and Grandpa Eddie certainly loved her mother. And as for her mother's parents, the Bainbridges—well, the Colliers rarely saw them.

Cameron had always taken it for granted that her mother's side of the family was distant—emotionally distant—because of the *physical* distance that separated them.

And her mother wasn't much of a family type, anyway. She loved her in-laws and was always a cordial hostess to them, but she wasn't into family holidays with big sit-down dinners and traditions. When it came to Thanksgiving and Christmas, she liked to take off with her husband and daughters. One year the Colliers had gone on a two-week Caribbean cruise for Christmas; another, they had spent Thanksgiving in Hawaii.

A few times, when Cameron's father's parents still lived in New York, they'd spent Thanksgiving there, watching the Macy's parade on Broadway.

But never, ever, had they spent a holiday with the Bainbridges. In fact, they'd only been to Georgia to visit them twice that Cameron could recall—once, when she was very little, for some great-aunt's funeral, and another time, when her grandfather was recovering from some kind of stomach surgery.

Then there were a couple of strained, occasional weekend trips to Florida, and that last time for her grandfather's funeral.

Her grandparents had visited the Colliers in Western New York exactly twice. The first time, Cameron remembered, was when her mother had had Paige, and everyone thought there was something wrong with the baby. She turned out to be fine eventually—she just had some kind of disorder that made her stop breathing in her sleep, which made her turn blue on a couple of terrifying nights. But Cameron's grandparents had flown up, and they had stayed in a hotel, and everyone had been grim the whole time they were there. Of course, that was probably because they were so worried about Paige.

The only other time they visited was when her grandparents went on some senior citizen trip to Niagara Falls, which was only an hour away from Weston Bay. The Colliers had

CAMERON: THE SORORITY

met them there for the day, and again, Cameron realized, there was tension in the air.

They were practically strangers, her grandparents, and she'd never known what to say to them. Even her parents seemed to have a hard time—especially her mother, who, whenever they were around, wore a tight smile and looked the way she did when company dropped by the house while she was working in her darkroom. It was like she was trying to be gracious, but she desperately longed to be somewhere else.

On the other hand, Lionel Collier was a natural at conversation. Cameron's father could talk to *anyone* about *anything*, a gift she supposed she herself had inherited. She recalled how he would engage her grandparents—who, like their daughter, invariably wore stiff smiles and spoke in overly formal tones—in endless small talk.

She had always *thought* the Bainbridges liked her father—who, after all, didn't like her father? But then, she supposed it was possible that her grandparents hadn't wanted her mother to marry him.

Because he was black.

It was a horrible thought, and it most likely would never have crossed Cameron's mind if it weren't for what her friends had said yesterday. About the Ku Klux Klan, and about people maybe not accepting Cameron because of her mixed-race background.

What if her own grandparents hadn't accepted her father? What if that was why her mother didn't want to see them?

And if her grandparents didn't accept her father, then they certainly couldn't be thrilled with mulatto grandchildren, could they?

It seemed impossible to believe that Cameron's liberal, tolerant mother could come from a racist household, though. Shelley Collier didn't have a prejudiced bone in her body.

No, surely Cameron's grandparents hadn't given her mother a difficult time over her marriage. Surely the reason for their distance was that they were simply—well, cold, formal people who happened to live hundreds of miles away.

In fact, Cameron thought suddenly, maybe she *should* look her grandmother up while she was down here. Maybe, since they were living only a few hours from each other, they could even visit.

It might be nice to get to know the woman who, after all, was technically as close to her, in terms of relationships, as Grandma Elma was. They were both her grandmothers, and everyone knew that grandparents loved you unconditionally.

The Bainbridges had simply never had a chance to build a bond with their granddaughters, Cameron told herself. But she was going to give her grandmother a chance to do just that.

As soon as Cameron was settled in, she'd give her a call.

Settled in.

Oh, Lord.

Her gaze went back to the stacks of clothing and bedding that were waiting to be unpacked, aired out, and put away.

She'd better get busy.

Chapter 3

"Kim?"

"Yeah?"

"Did I wake you up?"

"Cameron?"

"Uh-huh." Cameron transferred the phone to her other ear and leaned against the cinderblock wall, careful to keep her navy-and-white nightshirt pulled down to cover the tops of her thighs. Thayer Hall was a coed dorm, and despite the fact that the place wasn't nearly filled to capacity, and that it was late—way past midnight—there seemed to be people wandering around everywhere.

"What's up, Cam? You all right?" Kim asked groggily.

"I'm fine. Look, if you were sleeping—"

"Actually, I was. I went out to the Pines earlier, and I drank wine. Wine always makes me sleepy."

"Sorry. I figured you were the only one I could call at this hour." She knew Kim was usually up into the wee hours—she always had been, even on school nights. Besides, her mother, Suzy, was the only parent of her friends who wouldn't be alarmed or annoyed at a late-night phone call...*if* she happened to be at home.

"Hey, what's going on down there? Where are you?"

"At school."

"I know *that*, Cam. I mean, where are you calling from?"

"The pay phone in the dorm hallway. And I'm charging it to my parents' credit card, so I can't talk long. I don't get my own phone in my room until classes start next week."

"How come?"

"I have no idea. Everything's not quite up and running yet. Anyway, I just wanted to talk to someone...you know, from home." She lowered her voice as two semi-cute guys, both of them wearing shorts without shirts and bandannas around their heads, passed by her in the hallway.

"Are you homesick?"

"No way," Cameron said—and it was the truth. Mostly. "I'm having a blast."

"Already? Wow, I can't wait to get to Summervale. Did you meet a bunch of people to hang out with yet?"

"Well, I met a few people so far, at dinner in the dining hall. I ate with this girl, Lisa, and her new roommate, Valerie, who also just got in today."

"Are they cool?"

Again, Cameron lowered her voice—not that anyone was in the immediate vicinity, but the hallway wasn't exactly private. "Valerie is. She's from Atlanta, and she's going to major in education."

"What about the other one? Lisa?"

"She's okay."

"Yeah, right. I hear that tone in your voice."

"What tone?"

"You know. So what's her deal?"

"She's...you know."

"A bitch?"

"Not exactly. More like..."

"A geek?"

"Uh-uh. Shallow. And maybe a little..."

"Snotty?" Kim supplied.

"Exactly."

"So ditch her. Fast, before she thinks she's your best friend, and everyone else starts to hate you because they assume you're like her."

Cameron grinned. It was so great to talk to someone who felt and thought the same way she did about everything. That was the problem with the people here—at least, the ones she'd met so far. Everyone was so...different.

Even though Cameron and her high school friends all had distinctive personalities, they had a lot in common. It went beyond their hometown and school and lifestyle. It was—well, an understanding about the way things worked and the way things should be. They knew what to say and how to act and what was important and what wasn't. These new people just didn't connect on the same level.

"Cam?"

"Yeah?"

"Aren't you leaving something very important out of this conversation?"

"Like...?"

"The men, Cam! I mean, if you're going to drag me out of bed, you've got to at least fill me in on what the guys are like down there. Are they all a bunch of rednecks—or surfers? What's the deal?"

"I can't tell yet," Cameron said honestly. In the dining hall earlier there may have been a few rednecks, and a few surfers, too, as far as she could judge by looks and attitude alone.

"What do you mean, you can't tell?"

"The guys who are already here are here to Rush, so they're pretty much... you know, that type."

"Frat boys."

"Exactly."

"That's not a bad thing," Kim decided. "Frat boys can be pigs, but they're definitely fun. Have you hooked up yet?"

"I've been here less than twenty-four hours, Kim."

"And I'm asking if you've hooked up yet," her friend repeated earnestly.

"No. Not yet," Cameron said, smiling.

"Well, you'd better stop wasting time, then, girl. Start scamming."

"Yes, sir. Listen, I should let you go. Not that I want to... but it's only the first night. My parents will kill me if I rack up a huge phone bill so soon."

"Well, call me back when you have exciting news to report."

"I will. Tell everyone I said hi, will you?"

"Sure."

"Oh... how is everyone? What'd you guys do today?" Cameron asked belatedly, and a little guiltily.

"Allison and I went over to help Zara bring her stuff to UPS to ship to Dannon."

"Already? She doesn't leave for a few weeks."

"No kidding. You know Zara."

"I know. What about Bridget?"

"Didn't see her. She and Grant had something going today. As usual."

Kim's words held the slightest tinge of contempt, but it didn't escape Cameron, who said nothing. She knew Kim thought Bridget had missed out on a lot of fun in high school, having "chained herself to one guy," as Kim put it.

Cameron didn't know what to think about Bridget and Grant's relationship. She supposed they were limiting themselves by seeing each other so exclusively that they hadn't even planned to go to separate colleges. But then, it must be exhilarating to be so much in love that you couldn't stand the thought of being apart, even temporarily.

Now that she was settled at college—well, okay, not *settled*, but *at* college—Cameron decided maybe she was ready to fall in love...

If she had time, since she was going to be pretty busy with rushing and starting classes and making new friends....

Who are you kidding? You only wish you'd meet someone you could fall for.

Kim yawned audibly in her ear, and Cameron said once again, "I'll let you go."

"Okay. But call me again and let me know what's up, Cam. I'm totally jealous."

"You'll be on your way to Indiana before you know it."

"Yeah, I just hope I have as wild a time as you're going to have in Florida."

"What makes you think I'm going to have a wild time?"

"Have you ever *not* been a social butterfly?"

Cameron grinned and shrugged. It was so good to talk to someone who *knew* her.

The bandanna boys strolled back along the corridor just as she was hanging up the telephone.

"Hey, Yankee," the shorter one said in a thick southern drawl. "Did y'all tell your poor honey back home how much you miss him?"

She bristled at being called "Yankee" until she realized he'd pointed to the nightshirt she was wearing, which had a New York Yankees insignia near the collar.

"What's your guess?" she asked, raising an eyebrow at the

guy, who was pretty cute, if you liked longish blond hair, sunburns, and pierced ears.

"I guess y'all are telling the poor guy it's over, now that you've caught a look at *real* men," he drawled, gesturing at himself and his friend.

She smiled and tossed her hair flirtatiously. "Guess again," she said over her shoulder as she made her way back down the hall.

"Hey," the second bandanna guy, the taller one, called after her. "What's your name?"

"Cameron Collier."

"I'm Rhett. And this is Puny Petey."

"Just Pete," the short guy corrected, then muttered, "You dick," to his friend.

"Nice to meet you. G'night, boys," Cameron said sweetly and closed her door.

Okay, so Rhett and his pal Puny—Pete—weren't exactly her type. They were a little too cocky, a little too—well, unpolished. That didn't mean she might not want to hang out with them. And chances were, they had friends.

It couldn't hurt to cultivate as many guy-pals as she could, Cameron decided. Tomorrow, she'd make it a point to flirt madly.

She'd made plans to go to the beach with Lisa and Val and some of the other girls who'd shared their table at dinner. It was a little late in the season to work on a tan, but here in Florida, she supposed people sunbathed all year round. With her dark complexion, she tanned more easily than most of her friends. She figured she wouldn't have to work hard to keep some color.

She knew what her mother would think about that. Shelley Collier was always spouting off about the dangers of the sun, and how they should all be wearing, like, number two-hundred SPF lotion every day. But Cameron figured that since she didn't burn, thanks to her father's genes, she was pretty safe.

Cameron climbed into bed, turned off the light, and smiled into the darkness.

She was going to love college. It was just too bad that Kim and Bridget and Zara and Allison weren't here to share it with her.

"Hey, let's drive down Sorority Row on the way," Lisa suggested as she started the motor on her BMW convertible.

"Why? Haven't you seen it yet?" one of the girls in back asked impatiently.

Cameron wasn't sure of her name. It was either Mary Jane or Mary Jo, she couldn't remember which. She and her roommate, Bethany, were across the hall from Lisa and Val, who was also in the backseat.

"Of course I've seen it," Lisa said, "But I want to see it again. It gets me psyched for Rush Week."

As they drove down the quiet campus streets, Cameron looked around, scarcely able to believe that she was a part of

CAMERON: THE SORORITY

this place. It seemed like just two seconds ago that she'd been driving through campus in a rental car with her parents, full of wistful hopes.

"Which sorority do y'all want to pledge, Mary Jo?" Lisa was asking over the blaring car stereo.

"The Omegas, what else?"

"Me, too," Bethany piped up.

"Well, who wouldn't want to be an Omega?" Lisa cast a sideways knowing glance at Val and Cameron. "I mean, if y'all don't get into the Omegas, who do you want?"

"I don't care, just as long as their house is nice and they have good parties," said Mary Jo. She was a pretty, large-boned girl who, like Lisa, was from Alabama. But, as Lisa put it, Mary Jo hailed from "small-town Alabama, not Mobile." Obviously, there was a big difference—at least, as far as Lisa was concerned.

Bethany, on the other hand, was a sleek, sophisticated brunette who had grown up on Long Island. When they'd first met, Cameron had thought she might hit it off with Bethany simply because they were both northerners, but now she wasn't so sure.

Over lunch Bethany had proved herself to be even snobbier than Lisa. All she talked about was her friends back home, making them sound like some kind of Who's Who roster. If you believed her, she'd grown up playing with movie stars' daughters and dating billionaires' sons—not to mention visiting her "royal" cousins in Europe every vacation.

Naturally, Lisa lapped it all up and did her own share of name-dropping, leaving gullible Mary Jo utterly entranced. But Val had caught Cameron's eye as they were finishing their salads and shot her a look that said, "This is making me sick... how about you?"

Cameron knew she was going to really like Val, whose quiet way of speaking had at first made her seem a little standoffish. But she had a warm smile, and she was definitely smart—maybe even as smart as Zara. You could just tell by talking to her.

At first, Cameron hadn't thought Val was very attractive—probably because her light brown hair and makeup-free face didn't command attention the way Lisa's or Bethany's flashier looks did. But now she thought Val was naturally prettier than both of them. She just didn't choose to play up her appearance.

"There it is!" Lisa exclaimed, turning onto the wide avenue lined with large old houses. "That's the Omega house on the corner. Isn't it gorgeous?"

It was—a three-story white brick home with pillars and a wide veranda. The black shutters and wrought-iron railings gleamed in the sun; the lawn looked lush and the hedges were meticulously trimmed. Brightly colored flowers spilled out of planters beside the front door and hanging pots along the veranda.

"Oh, my God, I *have* to live there," Mary Jo said, practically clambering over the side of the convertible in her efforts to see the house. "It looks like Tara."

CAMERON: THE SORORITY

"Speaking of Tara, I met some loser named Rhett last night," Bethany announced. "He told me I was the most gorgeous woman he'd ever seen, and I was like, 'Get a life.'"

"I met him," Cameron said. "At least, I think I did. How many guys named Rhett can there be at Thayer?"

"This is the South, honeychile," Val said in an exaggerated drawl, smiling. "There could be dozens of them."

"Well, this Rhett was a real jerk," Bethany said.

"Really? My Rhett was nice, so he probably wasn't the same one," Cameron said, though *nice* was a bit of an exaggeration.

"Was he wearing a black bandanna on his head?"

"Yeah..."

"That was him. How could you think he was nice?"

"Because he was." She decided she *really* didn't like Bethany. "I mean, he was definitely a little..."

"Obnoxious?"

"No. He was a flirt, that's all," Cameron said pointedly.

"Well, I can't deal with people like that," Bethany said. "Oh, please... which house is that?"

"It's the Sigma house," Lisa said, making a face at the low, slightly ramshackle bungalow on their right.

"It definitely needs a paint job." Mary Jo giggled.

"It's getting one," Val pointed out, turning her head as they passed by.

Cameron followed her gaze and saw that a broad-shouldered, shirtless man wearing a backward baseball cap was perched on a ladder on the side of the house, dabbing a white-tipped paintbrush at the gingerbread trim above a window.

"Oooh, check out the bod on him," Mary Jo said. "And the tan."

"He's definitely yummy," Lisa agreed.

"*If* you have a thing for house painters," Bethany said.

"God, Bethany, are y'all always this crabby?" Mary Jo asked bluntly.

Cameron admired her for asking, but Bethany was unflustered.

"Always," she said cheerfully. "My friends at home call me Wench."

"I wouldn't go around bragging about that if I were you, Bethany," Cameron told her. She said it in a teasing tone, but she was thinking again that she couldn't stand the girl.

"Why not? Everyone loves a wench."

"Yeah, like Erica Kane on *All My Kids*," Lisa added.

"Right. I love *All My Kids*."

"Y'all do, too? So do I," Mary Jo said.

As it turned out, only Cameron and Val weren't big fans of the daytime soaps, particularly *All My Children*. While the others excitedly discussed Erica's latest double cross, Cameron stared out the window at the remaining sorority houses, imagining again what it would be like to live in one of them.

The very last one on the street, the Lambda house, was the most charming by far. It was a two-story clapboard house painted in what she was coming to recognize as Florida pastels—shades of pink and lavender with cream-colored trim.

CAMERON: THE SORORITY

The windowboxes overflowed with trailing vines and blossoms, and the winding flagstone path was bordered by a white picket fence. It was the kind of place where a person would have to feel right at home.

Well, maybe a *guy* wouldn't feel at home in such a decidedly feminine house. It had a cozy, female feel about it, but then, that was what sororities were all about, right? Sisterhood and all that?

Cameron decided, then and there, that she wanted to be a Lambda. They might not be the *crème de la crème*, as Lisa had put it yesterday, but they were definitely appealing.

At least, their *house* was.

She had yet to meet an actual Lambda, or any sorority girl here at SFC. So far, she'd only met freshman who, like her, were hoping to pledge.

"Yikes," Bethany commented as they swung around the corner past the Lambda house. "What's that supposed to be?"

"It's the Lambda house," Lisa said knowingly.

"Well, it looks like something out of the Brothers Grimm," Bethany said. "It's so geeky with all that...like, paint."

"Isn't it just," Lisa agreed, wearing what Cameron had come to recognize as her catty expression.

And just yesterday Lisa had been saying the Lambda house was one of the nicest on campus. What had she said? *"It's real charming."*

Cameron rolled her eyes and clung to the armrest on the door as Lisa rounded another corner, driving recklessly fast now that they'd left Sorority Row behind.

"Sun, surf, and sand, here we come," Lisa chirped, glancing at her own reflection in the rearview mirror and rubbing an imaginary smudge off her flawless complexion.

"Oooh, I love this song!" Mary Jo exclaimed as an old Gin Blossoms tune came on the radio. "Can y'all turn it up?"

"I hate this song, but since I'm such a peach..." Lisa jabbed the volume knob, and the throbbing guitar strains reverberated through the car.

They cruised past the quad, lined with its Spanish-style academic buildings with arched open walkways connecting them. Palm trees and flowering bushes made the whole area look more like a resort than a school.

Cameron tilted her face back, loving the feel of the sun's hot rays on her cheeks and the warm wind whipping her hair back. A carload of guys drove by in a Jaguar, whistling and honking.

Cameron grinned.

"What are you smiling about?" Val asked, her voice low in Cameron's ear.

"I just feel good," she said honestly. "Isn't this fun?"

"What?" Lisa shouted, as if they'd been talking to her.

"Nothing," Val and Cameron chimed together, then laughed.

As long as I make one good friend, Cameron decided, *I'll be happy here.*

Then again, why not hope for it all—pledging the sorority of her choice, and making dozens of new friends—*sisters*— and maybe even falling in love?

CAMERON: THE SORORITY

. . .

She should have known the day at the beach would be no day at the beach. The sky had turned overcast practically the second they'd spread out their towels, and within half an hour, an ominous thunderstorm had sent them scurrying back to the car.

The BMW seemed a lot smaller with the top up. They'd waited out the rain for a half hour, all the while listening to an incredibly boring, detailed story Bethany was telling about the time her brother had gone out with Princess Stephanie of Monaco, who reportedly was madly in love with him and begged him to marry her.

Finally they'd decided to call it a day and headed back to campus. As they drove by a strip mall—Cameron was discovering that there were a lot of strip malls in Florida—Mary Jo had announced that she *had* to have a frozen yogurt at a yellow-awninged place mysteriously called Y^2 & F^2. According to Mary Jo, it was pronounced "Y-squared and F-squared," and it stood for "Yogurt's Yummy and Fat Free!"

"If that isn't the most asinine thing I've ever heard," Bethany had said, laughing.

Privately, Cameron agreed with her, but she wasn't about to say it.

"Don't y'all have Y-squared and F-squared up North?" Lisa asked. "It's really big down here."

"No, we pretty much have *normal* places with *normal* names," Bethany said. "Like McDonald's."

"We have that, too," Mary Jo said, and even though Cameron was in the front seat and didn't turn around, she could almost see the smirk on Bethany's face.

It wasn't that Mary Jo was stupid, she told Val later, when the two of them were walking to dinner together. She was just a little—well, kind of airy. And... bubbly. Too bubbly for her own good.

"I know. The ideal prey for a predator like Bethany," Val said. "Did you see the way she jabbed Lisa when Mary Jo ordered that giant sundae with whipped cream and hot fudge?"

"No, but I overheard her and Lisa making fun of her wearing a bikini." Cameron shook her head in disgust. "So not everyone has a Barbie body like those two. You'd think they'd be a little more merciful."

"No, you wouldn't think that," Val said. "I know a zillion girls like them. In fact, I got stuck rooming with one last year. It was hell."

"You *roomed* with one? Aren't you a freshman?"

"Yeah, here. I meant in high school."

"You had a roommate? You mean you went to boarding school?"

Val shrugged. "Yeah. Why?"

"I don't know... I just never knew anyone who went to boarding school."

"But you know Bethany," Val said with a grin.

Cameron rolled her eyes. "Why didn't you chime in when

she kept going on and on about her private boarding school? She acted like the rest of us were bumpkins for going to 'day schools'—even Lisa, and her school was private!"

Val shook her head. "I don't care what Bethany thinks of me. People like her aren't worth it."

"Yeah, but don't you just feel like putting her in her place?"

"Who cares? Didn't you know anyone like her in high school?"

Cameron thought about it. "Not really. I mean, there were some people who were a little snobby, but no one in Weston Bay has a whole lot of money. Believe it or not, I was one of the better-off kids in school."

"Why 'believe it or not'?"

"Because ever since I got to school down here, I keep seeing people driving expensive foreign sports cars and wearing watches that cost more than what most people back home make in a month. I'm not used to being around so much money."

"Well, I am, and it's overrated. Most of the people I know have money, and most of them are miserable."

"How about you? You're not miserable."

Val tilted her head. "How do you know?"

"Are you?"

"Actually, not really. Not miserable. But I have my moments, thanks to my parents. My mother, really. My dad's not around enough to matter."

"Your parents are divorced?"

"No, that would be too messy," Val said in a mocking tone. "People would talk, and then there would be the lawyers and the financial settlement, and deciding who would get which houses—"

Cameron noticed it was plural. Not *house*. Val's parents must be loaded.

"And why bother with all that when you can just live separate lives? My father travels constantly for business, which means he doesn't have to deal with the evil Queen Eugenia."

"Who?"

"My mother."

"Oh. You don't get along with her?"

"I wouldn't say that. No, actually, *she* wouldn't say that. She's very refined, and she's probably never raised her voice in her life. So it's not as if we argue day and night. It's just..."

"You don't communicate anymore," Cameron supplied when Val trailed off.

Val laughed, and this time it was a bitter, unpleasant sound. "We've never communicated. But it's okay. How about your mom? What's she like?"

"She's great. A little flighty sometimes, and she's really hardheaded. But she and I communicate pretty well...about most things," Cameron added, thinking again about her grandparents. She'd never made a point of asking her mother why things were the way they were between the Colliers and the Bainbridges. But now she wondered what her mother would say if she asked.

CAMERON: THE SORORITY 63

"Do you think it's strange that a mother and daughter barely speak to each other?" she asked Val spontaneously, then realized it was a foolish question. "Forget it," she said hastily. "That's exactly what we were just talking about, wasn't it? How you and your mother don't speak?"

"We *speak*," Val said. "We just don't communicate. Why? Who were you talking about?"

"My mother and her mother. They don't seem to like each other very much."

"Nothing unusual about that. Most of my friends can't stand their parents. At least I'm civil to mine."

"My mom's civil to my grandmother, too. But it just occurred to me that in all the time I've been around, we've barely seen my grandparents. I just wondered if something happened between them and my mother."

"Like what?" Val asked, pulling open the door of the dining hall.

It was Cameron's turn to shrug. "I don't know. Do you smell..." She paused to sniff. "God, is that rotten eggs?"

"It smells like it," Val said, wrinkling her nose. "I always heard the food here was lousy."

"Me, too. So far, it has been. Want to walk over to that pizza place just off campus?"

"The one with the tables on the sidewalk?"

"That's the one. Let's go, before we bump into Lisa or Bethany."

"What? You don't want their charming company over dinner?" Val asked.

"Do you?"

"Duck—there they are."

"I guess that answers my question," Cameron said with a giggle as they hurried back out the door.

Chapter 4

The first official event of Rush Week was a tea at the Omega house the next afternoon.

"Nothing like starting with the best," Lisa said. She was lounging on Cameron's bed—uninvited, of course. She just had a way of seeping into a room when the door was open—and it hadn't taken Cameron long to get into the habit of leaving hers open. Everyone did, and people were constantly drifting in and out of each other's rooms. It was hard to believe they had only been at school for three days.

"*Start* with the best? I thought it was 'Save the best for last,'" Cameron couldn't resist saying.

"Well, in this case, it's definitely not true. The Omegas are the best. Which brings me back to my original question. What are y'all wearing this afternoon?"

Cameron towel-dried her hair. "My blue linen dress."

"Let's see it."

"It's not pressed yet," Cameron said, tossing her towel onto the floor. That was another bad habit she'd quickly picked up. It wasn't easy to be neat when you had a room to yourself and no parents around to tell you what a pigsty you were living in.

"Can I see it anyway?"

Cameron looked her in the eye. "Why?"

So you can make sure that your own outfit outshines mine? she added mentally.

"Because I was thinking of wearing blue linen, too, and we don't want to look like twins, do we?" Lisa asked sweetly.

"No, we don't want to do that." Stepping around a stack of jeans and leggings that was sitting in the middle of the floor, she crossed the room. She really should finish getting settled, she thought reluctantly. Her trunk was still half-full, but the dresser was crammed.

She figured she could sort through her wardrobe, figure out what she didn't need on an everyday basis, and maybe stash it in her trunk. She was planning to buy some cushions and turn the thing into a sort of bench seat—something she should definitely do before her roommate showed up. She didn't want the poor girl to think she was moving in with a slob of a pack rat.

"Here, this is my dress." Cameron yanked a hanger from the tiny, overflowing closet—more like a cupboard, really—and held it up to allow Lisa a fleeting inspection.

"Mine is nothing like that." Lisa sounded satisfied—and smug. "Yours is navy. Mine's lighter. But I don't think I'll wear it after all."

Cameron didn't reply, just laid her dress over the desk, which was still stacked with the sweaters she hadn't been able to fit into her dresser.

"Why'd you bring all those winter clothes?" Lisa asked, zeroing in on them.

"What, these sweaters? They're all cotton. It's not like they're wool or something." Dammit, why did she sound so defensive?

"Yeah, but you probably won't need them here. It's warm all year... and even when it gets chilly, it doesn't stay that way for long."

"Yeah, well, try telling my mom that," Cameron muttered. "You'd never know she grew up in the South. But maybe that's why she's always freezing, and she thinks everyone else is, too."

"She grew up in the South? Where?"

"Georgia," Cameron said guardedly. For some reason, she didn't want to talk about her family—not even casually—with someone like Lisa.

"Where in Georgia?"

"I forget the name of the town."

"What about your dad? Is he from Georgia, too?"

"No. New York City. How are you going to wear your hair for the tea?"

"I was thinking of putting it up, kind of like this," Lisa said, coiling her blond tresses on top of her head. "What do you think?"

"I think you look great like that."

Lisa smiled. "Really? You sure I don't look too sexy?"

Cameron kept a straight face. "I'm sure."

"Good, then I'll wear it this way. What about shoes? What shoes are you wearing with your dress?"

Good thing Lisa was so easy to distract, Cameron thought.

The tea wasn't what Cameron would call *fun*. How much *fun* could you have when you were standing around in a room full of polished antiques, nibbling crustless cucumber sandwiches with one hand and trying to balance a fragile-looking china teacup with the other, all the while trying to impress a bunch of blasé-acting upperclassmen?

It wasn't that the Omegas weren't nice. In fact, they were *very* nice, smiling politely and pleasantly making small talk as if they were sincerely interested in the hometowns and majors of a bunch of freshman nobodies, most of whom would never be asked to pledge the sorority.

Lisa and Bethany had their heads together most of the time, and they appeared to be assessing the other girls' chances of getting in. They giggled and jabbed each other a lot.

CAMERON: THE SORORITY

The sorority sisters had mingled, spending conspicuously more time on some girls than others. Cameron couldn't help noticing that they seemed to be avoiding the lone black freshman who had come to the tea, a stunningly beautiful model type. She'd caught two of the Omega sisters exchanging glances behind the girl's back, and she'd wondered, with a sickening feeling, what they were thinking.

She did her best to put the incident out of her head, but it tainted the rest of the afternoon for her. Not that it would have been terrific otherwise.

Cameron was sharply disappointed that the tea hadn't been more fun, and her cheeks and jawbone hurt from smiling so hard by the time she and Val were finally walking back down the perfect brick path, away from the perfect Omega house.

"What did you think?" Val asked as soon as they reached the sidewalk.

"What did *you* think? Let's go the long way around," Cameron inserted, gesturing up the block. "I want to walk by the other houses."

"Why? Because you've decided you never want to be an Omega?"

"Something like that," she said, and laughed ruefully. "It was pretty stressful, wasn't it?"

"I'd say so. It reminded me of one of my mother's little shindigs at home."

"Does she entertain a lot?"

"She's on the board of just about every charity in Atlanta," Val said. "She was also an Omega."

"So you're a legacy, like Lisa," Cameron said, surprised that Val hadn't mentioned it sooner. Then again, it wasn't so surprising, the better she got to know Val. She wasn't prone to boasting, that was for sure.

"I'm a legacy," Val echoed, but she didn't sound happy about it.

"Don't you want to be an Omega?"

"I don't have a choice. My mother has wanted me to be one since before I was born. She actually told me that when she was pregnant, she just knew I was a girl and that I'd grow up to go to SFC and join her sorority."

"That's unbelievable."

"Not really. Not if you knew my mother."

"What if they don't ask you to pledge?"

Val shrugged. "My mother will never get over it."

"How about you?"

"I'm sure I'll live," she said with a private smile that made Cameron wonder if Val would even be rushing if it weren't for her mother's expectations.

For a few minutes they were silent, strolling down the shady street and glancing at the sorority houses, most of which seemed fairly quiet.

It was uncomfortably warm and humid, and the heat radiated off the pavement in shimmering waves. Cameron's navy linen dress was damp and rumpled from the heat, and she could hardly wait to get home and strip it off, along with her panty hose.

CAMERON: THE SORORITY

"I wonder what's going to happen if Lisa doesn't get into the Omegas," Val said at last.

"What do you mean? She'll get in somewhere."

"I think so, too," Val said. "Lisa's really good at playing the role, did you notice?"

"If you mean did I see her buddying up to the sisters, saying just the right things and laughing just hard enough at their little jokes..."

"But not so hard as to seem indelicate," Val added, and they laughed.

"I can't imagine that the Omegas wouldn't want her," Cameron said.

"Well, if they don't, I feel really sorry for her."

"Why?"

"Because she has her heart and soul set on joining them. And she's a legacy, like me. I know her mother must be pressuring her, if she's anything like my mother. But the worst part is that Lisa's pressuring herself. The Omegas mean everything to her."

Cameron shook her head slowly, knowing Val was right. Lisa would be crushed if she didn't make the cut.

"It kind of puts things into perspective, doesn't it?" Cameron asked after a moment.

"What do you mean?"

"I mean, I want to join a sorority really badly. I left all my friends and my family and I came to school early specifically for Rush Week. I really want to live in one of these houses and wear a pledge pin and be a part of all the great parties. But I guess that if I don't get in, life will go on."

"Of course it will. But you'll get in, Cameron."

Surprised, she glanced at Val. "You think?"

"I *know*. You're bright and you're sharp and you're *nice*, which is a lot more than I can say for a lot of those girls."

"Too bad you're not already a sister, so you could sway the others for me," Cameron said, feeling warmed by Val's words.

"You don't need me to do that. I'll bet you anything you get in."

"Into the Omegas?"

"Do you want to be an Omega?"

"'Doesn't everyone?'" Cameron asked in a perfect imitation of Lisa's drawl. "No, actually, I'd like to be an Omega, but I wouldn't mind living there, either." She pointed at the Lambda house, which they were approaching.

"It looks like an upbeat place, doesn't it?"

"Definitely. I'm looking forward to the Lambda party tomorrow night."

"Me, too."

"Look at that corner room up there," Cameron said, stopping and pointing at the turretlike structure at the far end of the house. "Wouldn't you like to live in there?"

"Well, it's probably tiny."

"Cozy," Cameron amended. "It sure would beat my room at Thayer. I don't know how I'm going to fit a roommate in."

"*And* all of her stuff."

CAMERON: THE SORORITY 73

"I know. And my second trunk isn't even here yet." Cameron looked wistfully at the Lambda house. "Look, there's an attic. Maybe they'd let me stash my trunks up there. Or in the basement."

"This is Florida. There's no basement," said a masculine voice behind her.

Both Cameron and Val jumped, turning around to see a young man standing on the sidewalk.

"You scared the heck out of me," Cameron said.

"Sorry." He flashed a row of perfectly straight, white teeth at her.

He was, Cameron realized as she stared at him, one of the best-looking guys she'd ever seen. He wasn't that tall—maybe five-ten, around Val's height, which didn't matter because Cameron was only five-four, herself. But his build, evident in his clean white T-shirt and worn, faded jeans, was spectacular. His arms were muscular, his chest broad but not overly built up, and his waist lean. She'd bet he had a hard, flat stomach and that the muscles rippled.

And his clean-shaven complexion was dark—so dark he might be Hispanic, she realized, staring at his soulful brown eyes fringed by thick, dark lashes. His thick, straight hair was a bit tousled—not in a messy way; in a sexy way.

"How do you know there's no basement in the Lambda house?" Val was asking him.

"Because there's no basement in any of these houses," he said, and this time, his slight Spanish accent was evident. "But

I know this one the best, because I've spent the last two months painting it."

"*You're* a house painter?" Cameron asked, realizing he was the one they'd seen yesterday, when they'd driven by and spotted a cute guy on a ladder at the Sigma house.

"*I'm* a house painter," he confirmed. "What about me? You say it like you know me."

"We saw you yesterday," Val said. "We were driving by on our way to the beach."

"Oh, that was you?"

"You saw us?" Cameron asked. "In the silver BMW convertible?"

"BMW convertible?" He raised an eyebrow. "Now *there's* a nice set of wheels."

"They're not ours," Val told him.

"Well, I'm just kidding, anyway." he said, flashing that heart-melting grin again. "About seeing you yesterday. Do you know how many of you girls go driving up and down this street every day? Or even on foot, staring at the houses like some orphan who's wandered into the rich side of town. It's like they actually think that if they go by often enough, and if they look desperate enough, it'll rub off on the snobs who live in these houses and they'll let them in."

Cameron was taken aback by the dark glint in his eyes.

She didn't want to not like him....

Please don't give me a reason not to like you, she begged him silently.

CAMERON: THE SORORITY

But he definitely wasn't a big fan of sororities.

"So do you go to SFC?" Val asked casually, as though he hadn't just insulted them—in a roundabout way, of course, but it was an insult nonetheless.

"Yeah," he said, looking friendly again. "I'm a sophomore. How about you two? Wait, let me guess. Seniors, right?"

"Are we that obvious?" Cameron grinned at him, realizing he was kidding again.

"Yup," he said, smiling back. "You're freshmen to a T. But even if you didn't fit the mode, I'd think you were either freshmen, or transfers, because I've never seen you before."

"Come on, isn't this a huge school?" Cameron asked. "Aren't there, like, ten thousand undergrads here?"

"You'd be surprised at what a small world it is," he said. "And I never forget a face—particularly a really beautiful one."

Something warm oozed into the lower regions of her stomach, and she found herself practically batting her eyes at him—much to her vague disgust.

"What's your name?" Cameron asked, for lack of anything else to say.

"Tadeo Amata. My friends call me Tad."

"I'm Cameron Collier, and this is Valerie Armstrong."

"Nice to meet you," Tad said politely, shaking their hands with a warm, solid grasp, which was like something someone's parent would do. "You're obviously here for Rush Week."

"Obviously," Cameron said, her hackles rising. Was he going to make another derogatory comment?

"Why do you want to be in a sorority?" was all he said, rocking back on the heels of his Nikes with his thumbs hooked in his front pockets. Despite the benign posture, there was a challenge in his gaze.

"Because it'll be fun," Cameron said lamely, finding it frustrating to focus her thoughts.

Val said nothing at all, and Cameron remembered fleetingly what she'd said only a few minutes earlier about her mother—who was clearly domineering—wanting her to be an Omega.

"I guess if you like that sort of thing, it's fun," Tad said.

"What sort of thing?"

"Typical sorority stuff. You know, parties, secrets, rituals and traditions, and palling around with a bunch of loyal 'sisters'..."

"Who doesn't like parties?" Cameron retorted. "And what's wrong with loyalty? Sororities are full of girls—uh, *women*—who are upstanding citizens, excellent students, and—"

"Take it easy, Cameron," Val interrupted with a grin. "You sound like a spokeswoman for the Panhellenic Association or something. He just asked a simple question."

"Yeah, back off, Cameron," Tad said, but he was smiling, too.

She realized how fiercely she'd responded to his implied criticism of sorority life, and wondered what was wrong with her. Who cared what this—this *stranger* thought?

"Well, I'd better get to work," he said easily, pulling a Florida Marlins baseball cap out of his back pocket and planting it

CAMERON: THE SORORITY

backward on his head. "I have to trim the shrubs. I'm sort of an all-purpose Sorority Row handyman."

"You're working in this hot sun?"

"No choice. Tuition's due next week, right?"

"I guess." Cameron might not have been as wealthy as most of the other students here, but her parents were paying for college, and when it came to financial arrangements, she had no idea what was due, or when. Suddenly, looking into Tad's intense brown eyes, she felt incredibly naive.

He gave a little wave. "So, ladies, I guess I'll be seeing you around." He addressed them both, but he was looking at Cameron.

She felt that fluttery feeling inside again. "I guess we'll see you," she said stupidly. "Around. When classes start."

"Sooner than that," he said, "if you're going to the Lambda party tomorrow night."

She felt a fluttery rush of anticipation. "You'll be there?" she asked him, surprised.

"I'm bartending," he said. "It's great pay, and it's fun to watch everyone trying to have a good time while doing their best to impress the sisters."

"Well, *we* won't necessarily be trying to impress anyone," Val said lightly, "so maybe you won't have as much fun as you hope."

"There'll be plenty of pathetic wannabe pledges," he assured her. "Even if you two aren't among them. So listen, I'll see you."

"See you," they echoed in unison, then walked on as he headed up the path toward the Lambda house.

"What a jerk," Cameron said as soon as they'd rounded the corner and she was sure Tad Amata was out of earshot.

"C'mon, don't give me that."

She looked at Val in surprise. "Don't give you what?"

"You were so into him, Cameron. It was obvious."

"I was not into him!" Mildly annoyed, she shook her head rapidly as if trying to convince not only Val, but herself.

"And he was totally into you, too. I mean, he barely looked at me."

"He was into *me*?" Now that was interesting. Cameron glanced at Val. "How could you tell?"

"Couldn't you? The way he was looking at you, and baiting you? He enjoyed seeing you flare up about the sorority stuff."

"So who wants to go out with a guy who gets his jollies by pissing you off?"

Val smiled. "I never mentioned your wanting to go out with him, but obviously you do. And he was just teasing you."

"He was not. Didn't you hear him talking about sororities? It was like he can't stand them."

"Well, he had a point. People do act pretty—you know, pathetic during Rush Week. It's barely started, and even I can see that. Look at Lisa. And, God, look at Mary Jo."

Poor Mary Jo. She'd tried so hard at the Omega tea, chattering too loudly and too fast, and laughing too hard at all the wrong things.

CAMERON: THE SORORITY

"I wouldn't say she was pathetic," Cameron protested feebly. "More like... nervous."

Val shrugged. "Whatever. If Tad doesn't like sororities, what's the big deal? He has a right to his opinions, which are probably well founded. People *do* go nuts during Rush, and it *is* pretty ridiculous, when you think about it. You and I aren't taking this sorority stuff that seriously, are we?"

"Of course we're not," Cameron said. But she *had* found herself thinking that she'd be miserable if she wasn't asked to pledge. And that college wouldn't be much fun at all if she had to go through as an independent and live in the dorms.

What would Tad Amata think of that?

"Who cares what he thinks?" she muttered, causing Val to look sharply at her.

To her credit, Val said nothing and promptly dropped the subject of Tad.

But the rest of the way back to Thayer, as Cameron absently engaged in the debate about whether they should go to the dining hall or out for dinner, the dark-eyed guy with the cynical smile stayed on her mind.

"Happy New Year!"

Cameron blinked as a red-cheeked blonde swept over to the door, blew a noisemaker in her face, and plunked a pink and gold cardboard hat on her head.

"Welcome to the Lambda house," the girl said, planting a

similar hat above Mary Jo's ponytail and ushering them over the threshold. "Come on in. I'm Karla, and I'm responsible for coming up with the theme for tonight's party, thank you very much, not to mention making most of the arrangements. We're going to have a countdown at midnight and everything. Well, what do you think?"

She finally stopped talking as they stopped in the archway between the foyer and a crowded living room filled with people wearing party hats. The place was decorated with streamers, and tiny white Christmas lights were strung in the ficus trees that sat in a windowed alcove. An old B-52s song played in the background. The chattering voices were punctuated with toots from noisemakers and an occasional exclamation of "Happy New Year."

"It's incredible," Cameron said, taking in not only the animated party scene, but what was visible of the house itself on the fringes of the crowd.

Rose-colored brocade wallpaper and a floral border gave the room a Victorian feel. The antique-style moldings were a warm honey tone. A large pinkish-red brick fireplace was the centerpiece of the side wall, topped by a vintage mantel dotted with flickering white votive candles. Graceful parlor ferns and potted ivy, along with gilt-framed photos on the walls and tables, gave the place a homey ambiance that reminded Cameron of her grandmother's old Brooklyn apartment. There didn't appear to be any furniture—maybe they'd moved it out for the party—but it didn't matter.

CAMERON: THE SORORITY

She knew she had to live here. It was as charming inside as it had been out, and it wasn't just the house itself. The atmosphere was so much more comfortable, more laid back than the Omega tea had been. The girl who'd answered the door, Karla, had a casual, friendly smile and an easygoing attitude—you could just tell she wasn't a snob like most of the Omegas seemed to be.

She asked Cameron and Mary Jo their names, made pleasant small talk until the bell rang again, and quickly introduced them to two exceptional-looking guys before dashing to answer the door.

"Are y'all football players?" Mary Jo asked in her straightforward, bubbly way. She was practically drooling over them.

"I am. Jeff's not," said the beefier of the two, whose name Cameron couldn't recall. They both had a self-important air about them that eclipsed whatever personalities they might have had.

Cameron found herself tuning out the inane conversation they were carrying on with an effusive Mary Jo. Instead, she was looking around, checking to see what kind of people were here. They seemed to be mostly attractive, well-dressed, and having a blast.

Except for the rushing freshmen, who were as easy to pick out as midgets on a basketball team. They were the ones wearing the tight, hopeful expressions and trying to look as though they fit in when it was obvious they didn't.

She thought again of the word that guy, Tad, had used.

Pathetic.

Okay, so maybe he *was* kind of... well, right.

She found herself glancing around the room, looking for the bar—and bartender. Nowhere to be seen, but Jeff or his friend the football player would undoubtedly know where to find it.

"Excuse me..." Cameron cut into something Mary Jo was gushing, then said, "Oops, sorry, I just wanted to know if anyone has any idea where the bar is? I could really use a drink."

"Cool," said the football player, gulping the last swallow of beer from his plastic cup. "I'm empty, too. I'll go get you a beer... or whatever you want."

"That's okay," she said quickly. "I can go get it. Really. Just... where?"

"In the Florida room out back," he said. "Mind getting me a draft while you're at it?"

"No problem. Anyone else?"

The other guy, Jeff, shook his head.

"I'll have a sloe gin fizz," Mary Jo piped up, causing the two guys to exchange glances.

"Maybe you should go help your friend carry it," Jeff suggested to Mary Jo. "She only has two hands."

"It's okay. I can manage," Cameron said. "Anyway, we said we'd wait by the door for Val and those guys," she reminded Mary Jo, who looked only too happy to stay put in between the two guys.

They, on the other hand, didn't seem thrilled at the prospect of hanging out with a freshman chatterbox who'd made

CAMERON: THE SORORITY

the unfortunate choice of wearing a lavender plaid blazer that made her look two sizes bigger than she actually was, and who'd ordered a sloe gin fizz.

Cameron had no idea what that was, but she remembered a story she'd once overheard her mother telling a friend on the phone about the first time she'd gone to a bar, underage, of course. "The minute I ordered a sloe gin fizz, they asked to see my I.D. and then tossed me out," she'd said. "After that, I always drank chardonnay."

Great, Cameron thought as she shouldered her way through the mobbed living room and dining room. *Now I have to ask Tad to make a sloe gin fizz. He's going to think—*

Who cared what he was going to think? He didn't matter to her, not at all. He was too opinionated, too—well, not her type.

And besides, maybe he wouldn't be working tonight after all. That way she wouldn't have to ask him to make the sloe gin fizz. Good. She should hope he wasn't there, that he'd backed out at the last minute...

She should hope that, but she didn't.

Because she wanted to see him, and when she made her way through the kitchen to the screened-in Florida room and spotted him, she was charged. She didn't want to be, she shouldn't be, but she was.

He saw her, too. She *saw* him see her, saw his eyes dart in her direction almost as if he'd been looking for her, waiting for her.

When their gazes collided she expected him to look away quickly, in embarrassment or disinterest or whatever. But he didn't. He just raised his eyebrows, as if he were pleasantly surprised, and then he grinned. And waved. And beckoned her over.

Cameron's legs felt trembly all of a sudden, as she squeezed past a rowdy bunch of guys and covered the last few crowded feet to the bar. Tad was busy pouring beers for someone, and it gave her a chance to acclimate herself, and to remind herself that this—that *he*—was no big deal.

He was dressed in a black tuxedo, and boy, did he know how to wear one. *Debonair*, Cameron thought unexpectedly. It was an old-fashioned word she didn't use every day, but it sure described Tad right now. He may have been mixing drinks instead of mingling at a black tie reception, but he was definitely debonair about it.

She glanced around the Florida room, taking in the large banana tree plant.

The glass-topped table that was laden with bowls of tortilla chips, salsa, and bean dip.

The Japanese lanterns and speakers that had been set up in the yard, though no one was outside because of the bugs and humidity.

The cluster of white-painted Adirondack chairs where several girls—sisters, no doubt—were hanging out, three to a chair—one sprawled on the seat and two perched on the arms.

CAMERON: THE SORORITY

Cameron tried to act as if she were waiting patiently for her turn at the bar, which she wasn't....

Patient, that was. She fervently wished the two girls who'd asked for the beers would finish whatever they were saying to Tad, and she wished he didn't look so happy to be chatting with them. Couldn't he see that their stupid giggles were deliberately cutesy-pooh, like something out of one of those sixties beach bunny movies? Didn't he realize they were wearing too much of that fake tan-glo makeup?

Wasn't he as anxious to talk to Cameron as she was to talk to him?

Finally the two annoying gigglers had taken their beers and drifted over to the group by the Adirondack chairs. Tad instantly turned his attention to Cameron.

"What's up?" he asked, wiping off a spill on the bar.

"Not much. How's it going?"

"Okay. I'll be glad when this is over, though. The pants on this tux are too tight."

She couldn't help smiling. "Maybe you should find a seamstress to let them out for you."

An odd expression crossed his face. "My mother's a seamstress," he said slowly. "Who told you?"

"Huh? No one told me that. I just meant that if your pants are too tight you can—"

"No, I can't. The tux is rented."

"Oh, well..." She shrugged and tried to think of something to say.

"What can I get for you?"

She paused, trying to think. "A draft, and, um, I guess I'll have a glass of chardonnay...."

"Who's the draft for?"

"This guy I met," she said, lifting her chin and deciding he could think whatever he wanted about that.

"Oh." Something desolate flickered in his gaze.

"But he's not my date or anything...."

Shut up, Cameron!

"Just someone who needed a drink, and since I was coming to the bar anyway..."

God, what are you babbling about? Shut up!

But Tad was smiling, a faint smile that didn't reveal those even white teeth of his, but was sexy just the same.

"So you're here on your own?" he asked, pouring wine into a plastic glass and handing it to her.

"Sort of. I'm with my friend."

"Valerie?"

"Mary Jo. But Val's probably here by now, too. She was running late, so she's coming over with a couple of other friends of ours."

"So the gang's all here, huh?"

"Why do you do that?" Cameron asked, fortified by a sip of wine.

"Do what?"

"Get that sarcastic tone in your voice."

"Oh, that." He pumped the handle on a keg several times, then stuck a cup under the tap. "Sorry."

"For being sarcastic?" She wasn't expecting such a ready apology.

"Yeah. But, you know, like I told you, I'm not big on all this Greek stuff. I guess I just can't deal with people who are."

"So you can't deal with me, then?"

"I can deal with you. You're different." He set the foaming cup of beer on the bar in front of her, his eyes sliding up to lock with hers.

"Different from what?" she managed to ask and took another sip of her wine.

"From *them*," he muttered, tilting his head slightly toward a perfumed, hairsprayed threesome stepping up to the bar. "They're the types who'll flirt with a bartender, but only go out with the kinds of guys who drive Beemers and whose mothers *aren't* seamstresses."

"Oh." Cameron realized he'd been on the defensive earlier, that he'd assumed she was poking fun at his mother's job. She would *never* do that. *Never*. She realized how difficult it must be to be poor and work your way through a school like this. No wonder he was so prickly.

"Excuse me a second. Don't go anywhere," Tad said to Cameron before he stepped away to wait on the giggling gaggle.

She sipped her wine and guarded the beer and remembered that she hadn't ordered Mary Jo's sloe gin fizz yet.

As soon as Tad came back over to her, she said, "Do you promise you won't laugh if I ask you something?"

"Nope," he said. "I can't promise that. What if I think it's funny? What if I laugh? I don't want you thinking I go around breaking promises."

She smiled and contemplated that for only a moment before saying, "So you mean you're actually a guy who makes promises and keeps them?"

"I am."

"So, like, if you said you were going to call me, you would?"

"If I said I was going to call you, I would," he confirmed, not seeming the least bit taken aback by her blatant flirting. Good. She liked a guy who didn't get flustered.

"So will you?" she asked, swirling the mellow amber wine in her cup.

"Laugh?"

"No, call me?"

"I can't," he said, and she felt as if he'd kicked her in the face.

"Oh…"

"Not until you give me your number. Here." He slid a pink cocktail napkin and a pen across the bar.

She recovered in a flash and smiled, writing it down for him. "This is it," she said, "but my phone won't be hooked up for a few more days. There's some problem with the system."

"There's always a problem with the phone system in the dorms."

"Really? Which one are you in?"

CAMERON: THE SORORITY

"Which dorm? I'm not in one. I live off-campus," he added after a slight pause.

"Really? That's cool."

"Not exactly. I live with my parents."

"Oh…"

"And my four brothers and sisters. *And* a dog. In a three-bedroom apartment," he added with the air of someone who'd decided he might as well lay it all out there on the table.

"Wow," she said mildly. "Sounds pretty crowded."

"It is. But not as crowded as it would be in Cuba, where I was born. You don't know what it is to live like that," he said, a gleam returning to his dark eyes. It wasn't an accusatory expression, not exactly, but she had the sense that he was challenging her, that he didn't believe she knew anything about hardship.

"No, I don't know what that's like," she agreed. "But I've definitely lived in a crowded apartment. I was born in Brooklyn, and we lived with my grandparents in their one-bedroom apartment until I was three. I kind of remember it—my mom and dad used to sleep on the pull-out couch in the living room, and I had a little bed—I always picture it as one of those doll beds, you know, really small—it was near the doorway of the kitchen. And at night I would sneak in and grab a couple of Chips Ahoy—my grandmother always kept a bag in the cookie jar."

He was smiling, and she knew she'd won the subtle battle he'd staged. She got the feeling he'd been testing her. Now he knew she wasn't a member of the silver-spoon trust-fund brat pack that seemed to have hurt him in the past.

"So what's going to make me laugh?" he asked, leaning his forearms on the counter and ignoring the group of frat boys who'd just appeared at the other end of the bar.

It took a moment for her to track his thoughts. "Oh...I need a sloe gin fizz. For my friend."

He smiled. "That's okay. I'm stocked up on sloe gin. I see that you, however, are a sophisticated lady." He pointed at her wine, then grabbed a cup and plunked a few ice cubes into it.

"Actually, I'd rather have a beer," Cameron said honestly. "I was just trying to be impressive."

"Yeah? Well, don't worry about impressing a bunch of stuck-up sorority girls. They're not—"

"Not *them*. You."

His scowl seeped into a grin. "Me? You don't need to try very hard to impress me, Cameron. Just be yourself, okay?"

"You remember my name?" she asked in surprise, thinking she liked the sound of it on his lips.

"How could I forget? Do you remember mine?"

"Tadeo Amata. But everyone calls you Tad."

He looked pleased.

"Hey, buddy," called one of the beer-hungry frat boys. "We're waiting."

"Two seconds," Tad called, then said to Cameron, as he poured a draft into another plastic cup, "So what if I try to call you and your phone's not working yet? Will you think I broke my promise?"

"No. Because you don't break promises, right?"

"Right." He nodded and handed her the beer, taking the chardonnay away. "I'll see you before the night's over, okay?"

"Sure. See you."

As she balanced the three cups in her hands and pushed her way back through the crowd, she had to struggle to keep a big loopy smile from pasting itself onto her face.

Chapter 5

Three days and endless parties later—not to mention nights punctuated by constant fire drills, thanks to the dorm's anonymous practical jokers—Cameron and Val snuck off to the beach by themselves for some quiet time. Since neither of them had a car, they had to take the bus over, which meant transferring after waiting in the blazing sun for a half hour. They could have invited Lisa or Mary Jo, both of whom had cars on campus, but they'd decided it wasn't worth it.

"It's amazing how people can get on your nerves when you've barely known them a week," Cameron said as they spread their blanket on a vacant patch of white sand. "It's like I'm sick of those guys already. Aren't you?"

"Lisa and Bethany, yes. But Mary Jo's not that bad," Val said in her fair way.

"No, she's not," Cameron quickly agreed. "She just talks incessantly. It's like every once in a while you can't take it and you want to ask her to please be quiet for two seconds."

"I know. But you can't say that, because she's so totally insecure. She'd be crushed."

"No kidding. If she ever knew how Bethany and Lisa make fun of her behind her back..."

"I know, it's cruel," Val said, stretching out and opening a tube of sun protection lotion. She started smoothing it over her shoulders.

She was wearing a simple one-piece black bathing suit and gold-rimmed black designer sunglasses that must have cost a fortune, Cameron thought. She knew Val's family had bucks, but her friend didn't flaunt it. Her clothes were classic, well-cut, and conservative, and she wore them well. She didn't have Lisa's curvy, busty figure, but she was tall and had a willowy frame, and carried herself with a model's easy, long-legged stride.

Cameron had never thought of herself as small, but next to Val, she was practically a shrimp. And she couldn't help feeling a little flashy in her own floral print tank suit, which had reminded her of one of those Monet water lily paintings, and rubber beach flip-flops. As soon as she had a chance, she was going to buy herself a decent pair of sandals.

"I was glad you said something to Bethany that night at the

Lambda party," Val went on. "She deserved to be told she wasn't funny."

"I just couldn't take it anymore, the way she kept puffing her cheeks out and saying moo every time Mary Jo went over to the snack table. She's such a bitch."

"I agree."

"Lisa's not quite as lethal—she's actually kind of okay on her own—but I think Bethany's a rotten influence on her."

Val nodded. "I hope Lisa gets into the Omegas," she said, offering Cameron the lotion. "Want some of this?"

"I guess. I'm already pretty tan—"

"It's for protection."

"I know. I don't really burn much, but—"

"The sun down here is different than up North," Val told her. "You definitely need something. You've got a great tan, though. You're lucky you get such even color."

For a moment, Cameron thought about telling Val about her mixed background and that the reason for her dark-skinned complexion was that she was half African-American.

But before she could speak up, Val went on talking about Lisa. "You know, if she doesn't get into the Omegas, she's going to be destroyed. It's all she talks about."

"I know. She said she's not even going to the Sigmas' cookout tonight. She wants nothing to do with them."

"Well, what if the Omegas want nothing to do with her? I hope for her sake that she gets a bid from them."

Cameron nodded, spreading lotion over her thighs and

frowning when they seemed a little too jiggly for comfort. She'd been eating and drinking practically nonstop since she'd arrived at SFC, it seemed.

The dining hall food, which was definitely more convenient than leaving campus three times a day, was full of fat. They did have a salad bar, but it was stocked with the boring basics, and the only lowfat dressing was Italian, which, Cameron had learned the hard way, was too garlicky. So she'd been eating cheeseburgers and burritos and ziti, and now it was showing up in her thighs, and if she wasn't careful, she was going to end up overweight.

Never in her life had she had to worry about that, and it was a little disconcerting—particularly now that she was living in the land of tank tops and bikinis.

"So you're set on the Lambdas, right?" Val asked, flopping onto her stomach, facing the crashing waves.

"I'd love to get a bid from them. I wish you'd consider going with them, too, Val. We'd have a blast."

"My mother would—well, you know. I've got to go for the Omegas, Cameron."

"I know. I just thought the Lambdas were so much more fun—no offense."

"None taken. I'm not an Omega."

"Not yet. But you'll get a bid, Val. Anyway, of all the parties we've been to, the Lambdas' was the best by far. Don't you agree?"

"Yeah, it really felt like New Year's Eve."

Cameron flopped down on her stomach and smiled, thinking back to Saturday night. Just before midnight, the sorority sisters had started passing out bags of confetti and small, chilled bottles of champagne, and there were enough so that everyone got their own. Then there was a countdown, and precisely at midnight everyone shouted "Happy New Year!" and the room exploded in a riot of popping corks, tooting horns, and flying confetti. "Auld Lang Syne" played on the stereo, and everyone hugged and sang and some people even kissed.

Cameron had found herself looking for Tad, who was, of course, still tending bar. She wondered whether he'd be kissing her if he wasn't, whether he'd take her in his arms and lower his mouth over hers, and...

"Cameron?" Val said, as if she'd already said it a few times.

She blinked and looked at her friend. "Yeah?"

"Do you want to go into the water?"

"Nope, I'm not hot enough," she said, which was a lie, really. Thinking about being kissed by Tad Amata was definitely making her hot. But rather than cool off in the ocean, she preferred to be left alone with her fantasies, and she absently watched Val move gingerly down to the water.

Though she'd made two more trips to the bar that night, the party was growing more and more crowded, and Tad had been far too busy to talk. Her friends had wanted to leave after the midnight festivities, and though she'd made her way back to the bar to say a quick goodbye, her contact with Tad had been disappointingly brief.

He *had* said he'd call her, though.

Not that her phone in her room was turned on yet. She picked it up constantly when she was in her room, hoping to hear a dial tone, but getting nothing. She'd belatedly realized she should have given him the number of the pay phone in the hallway. She'd given it to her parents, who insisted on being able to reach her somehow.

But if Tad wanted to reach her, he knew where she lived. He could always figure out how to find her. Maybe he really didn't keep his promises.

Oh, stop being so paranoid.

She flipped onto her back and propped herself on her elbows, surveying the beach. It was getting crowded, now that it was almost noon. She saw quite a few lovey-dovey couples and a couple of Frisbee players who were obviously students at SFC, judging by their T-shirts. Two cooler-bearing mothers with a bunch of pail-and-shovel-toting toddlers passed by and settled a few yards away, setting up umbrellas and spreading towels on the sand.

"Brandon, come back here!" one of the mothers shouted, chasing after a towhead who was making a beeline for the surf.

Overhead, seagulls chattered, mingling with the pounding of the waves and the faint sounds of music from people's radios and the traffic back on the beachfront road.

Cameron was still having a hard time believing she was actually here, living in Florida, on her own at last. Not that she hadn't been a little homesick lately. But just a little.

And mostly because she missed her family and friends, not Weston Bay—or high school.

Maybe talking to her father on the phone this morning had made her feel wistful. One of his morning appointments had canceled, so he had used the extra time to call just to say hello. He wanted to hear all about everything Cameron was doing, and he kept making her laugh with his dry sense of humor.

Cameron had vowed, after hanging up, to spend more time writing letters and calling her family and friends. It was too easy to get caught up in life here, but she didn't want to lose sight of what was important.

So far, she'd spoken to Bridget once and to Allison twice, because Mr. DeMitri had interrupted the first call to make her go to bed, since it was past her "bedtime."

"You have to figure out a way to go away to school, Allie," Cameron had said when she'd called her friend back the next morning. "You wouldn't believe how great it is to have no rules."

"Oh, I'd believe it," Allison had said, sounding rueful. "But *you* wouldn't believe how hard it is to go to college when you have to pay for the whole thing yourself. I'm lucky I'm going to get to go at all."

"I'm sure you'll have a great time at State," Cameron had said quickly, feeling a twinge of guilt. What was the matter with her? She knew the DeMitris had no money, and that Allison would have to rely solely on financial aid and whatever she could make working two jobs and baby-sitting.

CAMERON: THE SORORITY

After that their conversation was a little awkward. Cameron hadn't wanted to go on and on about how great school was, because it might seem like she was rubbing it in. She would never, ever do that.

It was just so easy to get out of touch with the reality of Weston Bay, now that she was living down here with all these new people. People who were more worldly in some ways and less in others. People who were nothing like the friends she had back home.

Except Val.

Val would have fit in there, Cameron thought, watching her sleek form moving out into the surf. She was a regular person despite having grown up in Atlanta and gone to boarding school. Val didn't put on airs and she didn't judge people based on anything other than what they were like. With Val, it was simple. If you were nice, she liked you; if you weren't, she didn't.

Which was how Cameron tended to look at things.

Too bad the sorority business didn't work that way, too. Cameron had talked to quite a few of the Lambda sisters and she *thought* they'd liked her. Well, most of them.

A few, like Karla's friend Randi, seemed a little stuck-up. Naturally, Randi had hit it off with Bethany and Lisa right away, and the three of them had a grand old time whispering and nudging each other and wearing matching catty expressions.

Cameron had found herself secretly disappointed that not all the Lambdas were as affable as Karla had been, but she didn't want to let that taint her feelings about the group as a whole. Besides, maybe Randi and the few other snobby-seeming types weren't as bad as she'd thought. Maybe they just didn't make a good first impression.

She hoped so, because the Lambdas were the group for her. Now all she had to do was wait and see whether she'd made the cut. That would be evident any second now that invitations were going out for the next round of parties. The sororities only invited back the girls about whom they were serious.

An invitation to one of the upcoming events didn't necessarily mean you'd get a bid, but it did mean you could realistically hope for one.

Please let the Lambdas want me back, Cameron thought. *And please let Tad call.*

She wasn't sure which wish meant more to her—but maybe both would come true. Maybe she'd be asked to join the Lambdas, and maybe Tad would ask her out and they'd fall madly in love....

"Brandon! Leave the girl alone and get over here with that thing. Now!"

Cameron opened her eyes, hearing one of the frazzled mothers hollering in her direction.

A chubby-legged toddler stood over her, holding a juice box at a precarious angle over her head.

Before Cameron could react, he'd tipped it upside down, squeezed it, and sent cold grape-colored liquid cascading into her hair.

Sputtering, she sat up and reached for her extra towel.

"Brandon!" his mother shrieked, and came bounding across the sand.

She apologized profusely, and Brandon wailed, and Cameron assured them both that it was okay.

As she headed toward the water to wash off the stickiness, she told herself that the rude awakening from her dreams of the Lambdas and Tad wasn't a bad omen.

But deep down, she suddenly wasn't so sure.

You would think, when you sent a trunk by second-day-air delivery, that it would be there within a week.

You would think so, but you'd be wrong.

At least, you would if you were Cameron.

The rest of her belongings had yet to make an appearance at Thayer Hall, and the tracer she'd put out on the trunk hadn't yielded results yet. It wasn't easy to deal with the freight company's customer service department when you didn't have a phone where you could be reached.

Cameron no longer intended to give out the number of the pay phone in the lobby, since it was constantly in use now that more and more people were arriving in the dorm.

She managed to snag it the morning after the beach fiasco to call her mother and unleash her worries about her missing trunk.

"Don't worry," her mother said in her all-purpose reassuring voice. "It'll show up."

"But what if it doesn't? What if it's lost?"

"It isn't lost. It's probably just—"

"What? Taking a side trip to Europe?"

"You know I don't like it when you interrupt, Cameron, and I'm not crazy about that sarcastic tone, either."

"Sorry. I'm just really upset. I mean, my yearbook was in there, and all my family pictures, and my scrapbooks..."

"I know, sweetie. I'll see what I can find out. Do you have the tracer number and the eight-hundred number of the freight company?"

"Don't bother. I was on with them for, like, half an hour last night and they weren't much help. If it doesn't show up in another day or two, I'll have you call, though. You'll sound more official, and if they give you the runaround, you can yell at them. You're really good at that."

"Very funny. How's the rushing business going?"

"Well, I got invited back to an Omega cocktail reception."

"Is that a good thing?"

She remembered that her mother had never been in a sorority. "It's definitely a good thing, if you want to be an Omega. And most people do."

"But you don't?"

"I'm not sure. I'd be crazy not to go with them if they give me a bid. They're really exclusive, and everything."

There was a moment of silence on her mother's end of the line. Then Shelley Collier said, "Well, I hope they're a nice bunch of girls, too, Cameron. Because that's what's important."

"I know that, Mom. They're very nice. Don't worry. How's everything else up there?" she asked hurriedly, seeing a girl down the hall stick her head out of her room and look pointedly at the pay phone.

"Everyone's fine, except Hayley. She caught Paige's bug and she's miserable. Oh, and I bumped into Zara and her mother yesterday at Wal-Mart. They were buying some of those big cardboard under-the-bed storage boxes, and I was thinking about how small dorm rooms are. Maybe we should have gotten you some to take with you."

"Yeah, we should have," Cameron said, thinking of her cluttered room. "It's been a tight squeeze, and half of my stuff is sitting out in stacks on my desk."

"If I send you a check, can you get yourself to a Wal-Mart and buy a couple of those boxes?"

"Are you kidding? Sure, thanks, that would be great." It would at least solve part of her storage problem...which would only be compounded when—*if*—her other trunk materialized. Maybe it was better off lost forever.

"What did Zara have to say?" she asked her mother. "I haven't talked to her."

"She said she'd written you a letter, so you should be hearing from her."

"That was nice," Cameron said, feeling guilty that she hadn't called Zara. Of all four of her closest friends, Zara was the one with whom she had the least in common. Not that they weren't close, because there was no one whose advice Cameron trusted more—unless it was in the romance department, where Zara had little experience. And she definitely wasn't the person to talk to if you were thinking of cutting a class or making up sources for a term paper.

"She's excited about going off to Dannon," Mrs. Collier said. "At least, she said she was."

"She didn't seem excited?"

"Maybe apprehensive is a better word. I'm sure she's looking forward to it. And her mother kept talking about what a marvelous school it is...did you know she went there?"

Cameron rolled her eyes. "Yeah, I knew."

"I'm sure Zara will enjoy it."

"I'm sure she will. I just hope her mother lays off."

"Don't they get along?"

"They get along, but..." That reminded her. "Mom?"

"Mmm-hmm?"

"How come we never visited Grandma and Grandpa very often? Your parents, I mean, not Dad's."

There was a pause, and Cameron tried to imagine her mother's face. Was she biting her upper lip, the way she sometimes did when she was uncomfortable? Was she annoyed that Cameron was bringing this up? Or did she look sad, the way she did, once in a blue moon, when the topic of the Bainbridges came up?

Cameron had always assumed her mother was sad because her parents lived so far away, and maybe she missed them.

Now—especially the longer she waited for her mother's reply—she wasn't so sure.

CAMERON: THE SORORITY

"Why do you ask?" was what she finally said, effectively muddling Cameron's thoughts.

"I just wondered if, you know, there was a reason. Other than the fact that they live hundreds of miles from Weston Bay."

"Is it being in Florida that's making you think about Grandma? You're not thinking of visiting her, are you?"

Her mother sounded so worried at the idea that Cameron said, "No, it's not that. I was just wondering..."

"Why? Because you're down there? Or was it what we were talking about—about Zara and her mother not getting along?"

"I guess a little of both." Cameron shifted and pretended she didn't see the girl down the hall sticking her head out the door and looking at the phone again.

"My parents and I just weren't very... compatible, I guess, is the best word, Cameron. They're good people, and we loved each other. I felt terrible when my dad died...." She trailed off, then added, "And of course, your grandmother loves you, you know that, don't you?"

Actually, she hadn't ever really thought about it like that.

Love.

It was such a strong word. She *knew* that Grandma Elma loved her. She was always smoothing Cameron's hair and hugging her and doing things for her, like giving her the heirloom trunks, and giving her Milky Way bars, which were her favorites, and asking questions about school and her friends, so that you knew she was really interested in Cameron's life.

Her grandmother Bainbridge, on the other hand, was pretty much a stranger.

So it was impossible to compare, and just as impossible to think about *love* in a thought that contained an image of the white-haired woman with the stiff smile and the formal manners.

"Sure, Mom," Cameron lied. "She's my grandmother. Besides, I'm totally lovable, right? So why wouldn't she love me?"

She could picture her mother smiling at her little joke, and she could hear the smile in Shelley Collier's voice when she said, "She does. She's just—well, she's nothing like Elma."

"No, she's not. But we've always seen a lot of Daddy's parents. Maybe if we saw more of yours..."

She left the sentence unfinished, waiting for her mother to jump in and finish it for her.

But she didn't. All she said, after another brief pause, was "Why don't you tell me more about what you've been doing down there?"

"Oh, uh, I've been..." The girl down the hall stuck her head out again, then came out and motioned impatiently that she needed the phone.

"Listen, Mom?" Cameron said. "Someone needs the phone, so I've got to get off. We'll talk again soon, okay?"

"Cameron—" Her mother broke off abruptly, as if she wanted to say something but had changed her mind. "Take care of yourself, sweetie. I love you. Really. I love you so much, Cameron."

"I love you, too."

Oh, God, she suddenly felt like she was going to cry.

She hung up and bent her head as she walked quickly back to her room, passing the disgruntled girl who was rushing toward the phone.

Once the door was closed behind her, Cameron let the tears flow. They'd come from nowhere, and she had no idea what was wrong with her, but she cried and cried, noiselessly, sitting on her bed with her arms wrapped tightly around her knees, rocking back and forth.

Chapter 6

Funny, the way a day could start out so lousy and then get instantly better in the space of ten minutes.

This morning's unexpected crying jag had left Cameron in a blue mood that she finally attributed to homesickness. The sound of her mother's voice, and the realization that she was so far away, had hit her hard...and all at once.

She supposed it was normal, and that she was lucky she'd managed to avoid the wave of emotion for as long as she had. It had simply snuck up on her when her defenses were down and her emotions were close to the surface, thanks to the missing trunk, her worries over the sorority bids, and her brooding over Tad.

Some people, she knew, went away to college and were

CAMERON: THE SORORITY

miserable for months, missing home, failing to make friends and adjust. At least she didn't have that problem. She knew she'd get over this, but for now she felt like wallowing, so she did, feeling even more sorry for herself when she realized she didn't even have her mementos of home and the past—not even a photo of her family or friends—to help her feel better.

She skipped lunch—she could stand to, given the disturbing state of her thighs—and was lying on her bed, flipping absently through a copy of *Marie Claire*, when a sudden, shrill ring made her sit up.

For a second she thought it was yet another fire drill, but then it stopped just as abruptly as it had started.

What the hell was—

It happened again, and she realized it was coming from the phone....

The phone!

It was actually ringing.

Which meant that not only did it work, but that someone was trying to reach her....

Possibly Tad.

She lunged off the bed for it, thinking even as she did that it probably wasn't him and she shouldn't get her hopes up. She'd given the number to dozens of people in the past week. There was no reason to expect it to be Tad.

No, she shouldn't set herself up for crushing disappointment....

"Cameron?"

Oh-my-God-it's-him-it's-him-it's-him!

Her heart took off without warning, flying wildly into her throat, and it took her a second before she could force her voice past it.

"This is Cameron," she said in what she hoped was a casual —or at least *normal*, for God's sake—tone.

"This is Tad Amata. Your phone works. When did they turn it on?"

"I have no idea."

"It must have been just now, because..."

He trailed off and she automatically prompted, "Because...?"

"Because I've been trying to call you pretty regularly and it wasn't working a little while ago," he said, sounding a little sheepish.

A thrill shot through her as she realized the implications of what he'd told her. *I've been trying to call you pretty regularly.* That meant he'd actually been *anxious* to talk to her! Maybe even as anxious as she'd been for him to call....

Nah, probably not. He was a *guy*, and a guy was probably different. Besides, he was busy. He was working, and he lived with his family, and all that. He probably hadn't had time to sit around and wonder about her, the way she had about him.

"I'm really glad you called," she said honestly, then hoped she wasn't gushing like Mary Jo.

"You are?" He sounded glad, and his voice was more relaxed when he said, "Then maybe you'll be glad when I ask you if you want to go out tomorrow night. We could go see a movie or something."

"I'd love to!" she exclaimed, not even bothering to try sounding casual.

"You would? Great. I'll give you a call tomorrow, then, and we'll figure out what time and all that stuff. Right now, I've got to run. I'm on the phone at the Lambda house, and I've got to head back out and finish mowing before it rains."

She was humming when she headed downstairs to check her mail a few minutes later. And when she got to her box, she saw that there was actually something in it. A *few* somethings! That was a switch—she hadn't had much mail at all the past few days.

Cameron pulled out several flyers from local restaurants and stores, a catalog, and a couple of promising letters. She glanced at the first and saw that it was the one her mother had told her Zara had written. Then she flipped past it to the next envelope—and squealed.

The Lambda emblem was embossed on the cream-colored envelope, and inside was an invitation to their big dinner the day after tomorrow.

They like me!
Tad likes me!
Oh.

She suddenly realized that she'd done something really stupid. When she'd told him she'd go out with him tomorrow night, she'd completely forgotten about the Omega cocktail reception.

Now what was she supposed to do?

She had to tell him it was a bad night, and that they could go out some other time. But there wasn't really another good time in the near future—the Lambda dinner was the next night, and there were a bunch of other rush events this week. She didn't want to wait forever to see Tad, though.

And besides, something else kept flashing through her mind. For some reason, she kept remembering the look the two Omega sisters had exchanged behind the beautiful black girl's back.

"Hey, Cameron, what's up?"

She looked up and saw Mary Jo. She was holding her mailbox key and had an anticipatory look on her face, about to open her box.

"Hi, Mary Jo. I haven't seen you since yesterday morning. Where've you been?"

"Oh, around. I was just kind of bummed," she said, putting the key in the lock.

"What happened?"

"I didn't get an invite to the Omega party. I know they already went out."

"Oh, that's—"

"It's okay," she said, opening her box. "I'm over it now. At first I was crushed, but you know, they weren't that much fun, anyway. Did y'all get invited?"

She wanted to lie, but she didn't dare, knowing Mary Jo would find out eventually. "Yeah, I did. But I'm really not looking forward to it," she added hastily.

"Why not? It's all Lisa and Bethany have been talking about. Even Val got invited, and she's so quiet—not that she's not nice, and everything. I think I'm, like, the only one who didn't get asked to go."

"No, you're not," Cameron assured her, hating the conspicuous look of anguish on her face.

"What if I can't get into *any* sorority? What if no one wants me to pledge?"

"Don't say that, Mary Jo," she told her swiftly, as though it was the most ridiculous thing she'd ever heard. "Of course you'll be asked to pledge."

"By who? I'm starting to feel paranoid, like no one likes me. And most of the second-round invitations for the closed parties are already out. I haven't gotten any. What do y'all have there?" she asked, peering at the envelopes in Cameron's hand.

"Oh, a letter from my friend back home, and...uh, an invitation to the Lambda dinner—"

"They're out? Hey, maybe I got one, too. What else do y'all have?"

"Hmm? Oh..." She realized she had another invitation to open, this one in a teal-colored envelope that was a bright enough shade to be a little tacky. She knew, even before she opened it, what it contained.

"It's the Sigmas—wow, they're having a pig roast!" Mary Jo announced, reading over her shoulder. Her voice grew wistful. "That sure sounds like such fun, doesn't it?"

"Yeah," Cameron said, trying to muster some enthusiasm. "It sure does."

"Hey, look!" Mary Jo exclaimed, finally turning and pulling her own mail out of her box. "I got one, too!"

For a second, she sounded so thrilled Cameron thought she might be talking about the Lambdas' dinner. But she was waving a teal envelope, smiling so broadly Cameron could see her pink gums.

"I'm so happy for you, Mary Jo," she said sincerely. "That's great."

"We can go together."

"Sure..."

"Maybe we'll both be asked to pledge. Then we can be sorority sisters. I really liked the Sigmas' house. It was a lot more relaxed than the other ones, didn't you think?"

"Mmm-hmm."

"Did y'all get invited to the Alphas' carnival?" Mary Jo asked. "Because Val and Bethany both did. Lisa didn't. Me, either, obviously."

"Well, I didn't either. But it's no big deal."

She hadn't realized Val had been invited to the big Alpha event. It made sense, though. Alpha girls came from big, big bucks.

Val hadn't mentioned the invitation, probably because she knew Cameron hadn't been asked.

She felt a little pin-prick of consternation, identifying, only briefly, with the left-out expression on Mary Jo's face.

Then she realized that she didn't particularly want to be an Alpha anyway. So it didn't matter, right?

CAMERON: THE SORORITY

Right.

"Then, how many invites did y'all get to the closed parties?" Mary Jo was asking.

"Three," she said absently.

"I only got one. So far."

Cameron didn't tell her that the Lambda party was the last of the second round—all the other sororities had issued their invitations already.

Mary Jo asked, "Are the Lambdas still your number-one choice?"

"You bet."

"Their dinner is going to be a lot of fun tomorrow night, huh?"

"Definitely."

Her mind wandered back to Tad.

She didn't have his phone number. She had to find him and tell him, in person, that she'd accidentally forgotten she had other plans tomorrow night. But something told her he wouldn't be thrilled to hear she planned to blow him off in favor of going to a sorority dinner.

"What do you mean, you're not going to go?" Lisa stared at her, looking horrified.

"I mean, I have other plans."

"What could be more important than the Omega cocktail party? Do y'all know how many people on this campus would kill for a chance to go? Y'all can't just not show up."

"I have a date," Cameron told her, dumping another packet of sugar into her steaming cup of coffee. She'd taken a liking to the stuff ever since she'd tasted it on the plane that day. Well, maybe not a *liking*, but it helped her to wake up every morning after late nights and too many beers.

"A date?" A flicker of interest came over Lisa's tanned face. "With who?"

"You don't know him." She looked around the dining hall, hoping to see someone else she knew so that she could cut the conversation short. But it was pretty sparsely populated, except for Rhett, whom she was actively avoiding these days. He seemed to have taken a liking to her. Meanwhile, Mary Jo, for God knew what reason, had a fierce crush on Rhett.

"How do y'all know I don't know this guy, Cameron? I know a lot of people. Is he living at Thayer?"

"No." She stirred the coffee, decided it was too dark, and reached for another creamer.

"Is he in one of the frats?"

"Uh-uh."

"An upperclassman?"

"Are you going to eat both halves of your bagel?"

"Yes. And it was the last poppy one they had."

Bitch, she thought as Lisa finished smearing it with cream cheese and took a huge bite. She knew Cameron loved poppy seed bagels. Not that Cameron really wanted one right now, anyway. She was just trying to distract Lisa, which, she should have learned by now, was futile.

"So he's an upperclassman? That's cool. Where'd y'all meet him?" Lisa asked when she'd finished chewing and swallowed.

"Around campus."

"What's his name?"

"Tad."

"Tad what?"

"Geez, Lisa, what're you trying to do, pinch-hit for my mother? Hey, look, there's Rhett." She waved and smiled really big at him, which went to show how desperate she was to get Lisa off Tad's trail.

"Oh, gross. I can't stand him," Lisa said, pushing her chair back as Rhett headed in their direction. "I'm finished. Y'all can have the rest of my bagel after all. See you."

"Hey, Lis', nice shirt," Rhett said as she shoved her way past him. "It really accentuates your rack."

"Y'all are such an ass," she retorted, storming away.

"It was a compliment!" he called, then threw his hands up and looked at Cameron as if to say *what's the problem?* He plopped himself down in the chair Lisa had just vacated and said, "Can I have the rest of your bagel?"

"It's not mine, it was Lisa's. Knock yourself out."

"What are these little black things?" Rhett asked, poking suspiciously at it.

"Those? I think they're tiny dead bugs," she said, and sighed when he bit in anyway. "You idiot. They're poppy seeds."

"Huh?"

"Never mind."

"Where's your breakfast?"

"This is it," Cameron said, gesturing at her coffee.

"What, are you on a diet?"

She felt her cheeks grow hot instantly. "Why?"

"No reason. I mean, you're not fat or anything. I like girls who aren't rails."

Cameron thought of Mary Jo.

Then she thought of herself. She sipped her coffee and wished she'd only used one creamer instead of three. Maybe she should go over to the infirmary and get weighed. She felt like she'd gained weight, and her clothes seemed a little tight. She'd heard about the "Freshman Fifteen"—slang for the excess poundage people tended to gain their first year away at school.

But classes hadn't even started yet. If she'd gained weight already, where was she going to be by next May? Shopping in the Plus Sizes department at Nordstrom?

"I think I'm gonna pledge the Phi Kappas," Rhett told her with his mouth full. There was a smear of cream cheese on his cheek.

"That's great," she said, thinking he'd fit right in there. The PKs were the most clichéd fraternity on campus, like something right out of the movie *Animal House*.

"How about you?" he asked. "You closing in on the sorority of your choice?"

"I've got a few irons in the fire," she told him.

"Which way are you leaning? No, let me guess. The Omegas."

CAMERON: THE SORORITY

"Why do you say that?"

"They're the classiest, and you're a classy babe. Right?"

She brightened. "You think I'm classy?"

"Yeah. Not as classy as Bethany—"

"Gee, thanks a lot."

"Naw, she's a bitch, so it doesn't matter. You, you're not a bitch."

"Thanks," she said again.

"Want to go out with me?" he asked. "I can be classy, too. I can take you someplace nice. I've got my Saab. We can go down to Miami or something."

"Thanks, Rhett, but actually, I'm seeing someone already."

That was pushing it, Cameron thought, but it was partly true.

"Who? You got someone back home?"

"No, actually, he's here."

"Yeah? How come I never see you with him?" he asked, a suspicious gleam in his eyes.

"I haven't been seeing him very long."

"Well, then, it's no big deal if you go out with me, too."

"Yes, actually, it is a big deal. See, I haven't been seeing him for very long, but we're... we're pretty serious."

What was she talking about? She was out of her mind, telling someone like Rhett that she was serious with Tad when she hadn't even gone out with him yet. What if it somehow got back to Tad?

Not that Tad and Rhett could possibly travel in remotely

the same circles. Besides, the campus was enormous. And maybe by the time word got back to Tad, they really would be serious.

The thought sent quivers through Cameron's stomach.

She extricated herself from a persistent Rhett and made her way back to Thayer to wait for Tad's call and count down the hours until tonight.

"You look hot" was the first thing Tad said when she met him in front of Thayer.

Oh, God. Maybe she shouldn't have worn head-to-toe black, which wasn't exactly appropriate for Florida in late summer.

"I'll be fine. It's supposed to cool off once the sun goes down," she told him.

"No..." He grinned. "I meant you look *hot*. You know... sexy."

"Oh..." She felt her cheeks grow red. "Thanks," she said awkwardly.

But she was grateful he'd noticed. She'd actually spent over two hours getting ready for tonight, racing back and forth between Val's and Lisa's room and her own, borrowing earrings and liquid eyeliner and asking for advice on which shoes she should wear with her figure-hugging black shift. Val was helpful, as she'd expected, but Lisa kept telling her she was crazy to be choosing *any* guy over the Omega party.

CAMERON: THE SORORITY

"You realize this means you're not going to get a bid from them, don't you?" Lisa had asked more than once.

Cameron had told her that yes, she realized that. And it didn't matter to her.

Which was a lie, because it actually *did* matter. She knew she was taking a huge chance. She didn't necessarily want to be an Omega, but if no one else asked her to pledge, she would always wonder if they might have if she'd only gone to their party. And she'd be forced to go through college on the outskirts of the social scene, left out of the sorority life she'd so desperately wanted to be a part of.

On the other hand, she had been forced to choose between the Omegas and Tad, and she'd done the only thing she could do. She'd been ninety-nine percent sure that if she'd told him she couldn't go out with him because there was an Omega party the same night, he wouldn't have asked her out again.

Now, looking at him, beyond handsome in his baggy blue chinos and a plaid dress shirt in pale tones of beige and cream, she knew she'd made the right choice. She wanted to see where this would lead.

"My car's parked in the lot behind the science complex," he said. "It's a bit of a walk."

"That's okay," she said, glad she'd taken Val's advice and worn her most comfortable black linen flats.

"It's this way," he said, and they started walking. He asked her about Val and whether she'd registered for classes yet, and then he asked what her schedule was like when she told him she had registered.

"A lot of afternoon classes," she said, "which is good."

"Yeah, definitely. Especially if you plan to have an active night life, if you know what I mean."

He bobbed his eyebrows suggestively and she knew he was teasing, but her breath caught in her throat a little.

"I only have to get up really early on Wednesdays, for a lab," she told him. "So it'll be good."

"Yeah, that'll be good. I have to get up early every day. All the classes I need for my major seem to be first thing in the morning."

"What's your major?" she asked, realizing she didn't even know that basic fact about him.

"Political science."

"Really? What do you want to do?"

"Become a congressman and change how people are forced to live," he said promptly, as though he'd said it a thousand times before.

"Seriously..."

"I am serious. I want to make a difference, Cameron. Do you know how many people are just barely existing? Do you know how screwed up our government is, how they spend all their time and money worrying about the wrong things, things that don't matter?"

She was a little taken aback at the urgency in his voice. "I know," she said. "And if you want to make a difference, that's great. I mean... I'll vote for you. Got any bumper stickers?"

He cracked a smile, and she was relieved. She didn't feel like getting into anything heavy. Especially when she didn't feel entirely knowledgeable when it came to politics. Suddenly she wished she'd spent more time paying attention in Ms. Handelman's current events class last year, and less time forging passes so that she could cut with Kim.

Well, when classes started next week she would definitely make it a point to pay attention and study. Maybe she should start reading the newspaper or watching the evening news, too. She didn't want Tad to think she was an idiot.

"What about you?" he was asking. "What are you going to major in?"

"Oh... I'm not sure yet."

"Well, you don't have to declare a major this year, anyway. But which direction are you leaning in?"

"Uh, I really like photography," she said, realizing it was too late to escape the idiot factor on this date.

"Photography? That's cool. So you could get into journalism, be a photojournalist. You could travel around the world and take pictures of starving children in Africa and of the devastation in Iraq, and you could make people see what's going on beyond their own safe little worlds."

"Sure, I could do that," she agreed, feeling way, way out of her league.

The truth was, she wasn't sure she'd *want* to go to Africa and see starving children herself. It would be so upsetting. And what about wild animals? She hated snakes. And what about the Ebola virus? What if she caught that?

She didn't tell Tad what she was thinking, though. Instead, she changed the subject, asking him what he'd been doing the past few days.

"Working," he said. "Nonstop. I've been doing some hauling for my father's boss, and I finished painting the trim on the Sigma house this afternoon."

"What I've seen so far looks good, but not as nice as the Lambda house. That's the prettiest house on Sorority Row."

"You're kidding, right?"

"No, actually, I'm not. I think it looks cool, with all those pastels and that elaborate trim."

"An old-fashioned girl." He smiled. "Do you know how many people think the Lambda house is a big frou-frou joke?"

"I like Victorian gingerbread-y stuff," Cameron said lamely. "I think it's nice. Nicer than streamlined modern boxes, anyway."

"That's good. I think it's nice, too," he said. "Although pink isn't exactly my favorite color."

"What is?"

"Well, I used to think navy blue—but tonight, I'm leaning toward black," he told her, motioning at her dress.

She felt all warm and gushy inside.

"So, did you get invited back to the big dinner tomorrow night?" he asked.

"Yeah," she said hesitantly. "I did."

CAMERON: THE SORORITY

"But I guess you're pretty bummed about not being asked to the Omega reception tonight, huh?"

Her eyes widened and she stammered before managing, "I...actually, I did get asked."

It was his turn to look surprised. "You did? Then what are you doing here with me?"

For only the briefest moment, she considered telling him the truth—that she'd made a mistake, and had forgotten all about the Omega party when she'd accepted his invitation.

Then she heard herself saying, "I thought it sounded like more fun to be with you."

He broke into a broad, pleased grin. "You must be the first person in the history of this campus to blow off an Omega party."

"Yeah, well, I didn't want to join, anyway."

"Why not?"

"They're too stuffy."

"So you've seen the light. I'm really glad to hear it, Cameron. I figured sooner or later you'd realize that all this sorority stuff is a waste of time."

She stopped walking. "I didn't say that."

"You said you dropped out of rushing."

"No, I didn't. I said I didn't go to the Omega party." And she was beginning to wonder if she'd made a mistake.

"You're still going to join a sorority?"

"If I get asked to pledge, yes."

He shrugged. "Whatever."

They started walking again. Cameron tried to think of something to say, but she didn't want to argue with him, and everything that popped into her head was an angry response to his attitude problem when it came to rushing.

Finally he said, "Look, Cameron, I guess you know where I stand on this Greek stuff—"

"I guess I do," she muttered.

"And that's not going to change. I think you should try to enlighten me, though, because I don't think I get why someone like you thinks she needs to get into a cliquey bunch of snobs in order to get through college."

Okay, he was willing to listen. She had to hand him that. She fought to keep frustration and anger out of her voice.

"First of all, Tad, they do a lot of good. Like, the Lambdas have a project volunteering at a runaway shelter. And they have a canned goods drive at Thanksgiving, and they go sing Christmas carols at Shady Meadows—"

"What the heck is Shady Meadows? Sounds like a pet cemetery."

She saw that he was joking, and smiled. "It's a convalescent home. My point is, you have to remember that they're not all cliquey bunches of snobs. They really care about others."

"I wouldn't expect anything less from loyal *sisters*," he said, then quickly added, "I'm sorry. I guess I should tell you where I'm coming from, Cameron."

"Why don't you?" She was taken aback by his abrupt change from scornful to contrite in the space of two seconds.

"I've been doing odd jobs around the Lambda house and other places on sorority row for almost a year now, but only because I really need the money, they pay pretty well, and work is hard to come by around here. So I swallow my pride—"

"You don't have to swallow your pride just because you're working, Tad," Cameron cut in. "I spent time this summer working, too, to earn money for college." Okay, *spending* money, she thought, to supplement what her father would be depositing into her checking account every week, but still... "I babysat, and I was a lifeguard at this pool...." She eliminated the fact that the pool had been at her parents' country club.

"That's not what I'm talking about. Back at the beginning of last semester, when I first started working at the Lambda house, I overheard two of the sisters talking about me while I was edging the grass. I guess they figured I didn't speak English, or maybe they didn't care whether or not I overheard them, but they were saying that they thought I was good-looking and all that...." He looked uncomfortable.

"You *are* good-looking," Cameron said with a smile.

He didn't smile back. "And they said that it was too bad I was off limits."

"Why?" She was afraid of the answer.

"Because I was just a lowlife spick gardener."

Shocked, Cameron glanced at his face and saw the stark pain in his eyes. She didn't know what to say.

Finally she spouted, "Did you tell them you heard them? And that you're a student at SFC?"

"Do you think that would matter? Do you think I even cared what they thought, anyway? That I would give racists like them the time of day?" His voice escalated. "You don't know what it's like, Cameron. You come from a white-bread world just like they do. You don't deal with racism. You don't get what a problem it is."

She suddenly felt like she was going to... she didn't know what. Be sick, or burst out crying, or start hollering back at him. But what would she say?

That she *had* dealt with racism? It wasn't true, not exactly—except for those few isolated incidents in her past. And though she had felt bad about them at the time, they hadn't stayed with her. She hadn't grown up feeling different from anyone else.

Was now the time to tell him about her mixed-race background? That her father was an African-American who knew, just as well as Tad did, what it felt like to be the object of hate, simply because of the color of his skin—something he couldn't help.

Not that Lionel Collier had ever spent much time telling his daughters what it was like for him, growing up black in a predominantly white world. But Cameron was aware of her father's fierce sense of pride in his heritage—he had told them stories about how his family had escaped slavery and come North by the Underground Railroad back in the eighteen-hundreds. And as a child, he'd gone, with Grandma Elma and Grandpa Eddie and his sister, Aunt Ruth, to civil rights rallies. He'd heard Martin Luther King, Jr., speak.

"I'm sorry, Cameron," Tad was saying, and she turned blindly toward him. "I didn't mean to shout at you. It's not your fault. You have nothing to do with this."

"No, I don't," she managed to say, dragging her thoughts back to the present, to this troubled guy who shouldn't matter to her, because he was nearly a stranger. And yet he *did* matter, and she didn't want to walk away even though it would probably be easier than getting further entangled with him.

"I just can't believe you'd want to align yourself with a group like that," he said, shaking his head. "I just wonder if you know what it's all about."

"I know that it's about support, and friendship, and tradition, and having fun," she said. "I mean, that's what I want to get out of sorority life. And I'm not a racist, Tad—"

"I didn't say you were—"

"And I don't think the Lambdas are a racist group."

"How do you know?"

"Because they..." She fumbled for the right answer, not wanting to inflame him again. "Okay, maybe there are one or two girls in the sorority who aren't exactly... tolerant." She knew even as she said it that it was an understatement, given the cruel slander he'd overheard. "Maybe there are a few racists," she revised hastily, before he could speak. "But that doesn't mean the whole group thinks the same way. And it's not a good enough reason for me not to want to join."

"I guess it isn't, for you," he said with a shrug.

Again, she tried to find the words to tell him that he was seeing her wrong.

"Here's my car," he said then, stopping in front of a two-door, several-years-old blue Chrysler convertible. It looked newly washed, so clean that it actually gleamed in the fading sun. Inside, it was spotless, she saw when Tad opened the door for her.

"It smells so good in here," Cameron told him. "Like cinnamon or apples or something."

"That's the air freshener. I bought the car used, a few years ago, from a smoker. I finally got the smell out...almost. Do you want me to put the top down?"

"Yeah, that'll be fun."

He hesitated, his hand on the lever. "But what about your hair?"

"What about it?"

"It looks really nice. Like you spent a long time getting it piled on top of your head like that."

She had, and Lisa had helped her, using about twelve dozen bobby pins.

"It's no big deal," she told him honestly. "The wind will feel good."

He looked so pleased that she thought he was going to lean over and kiss her right then and there. But he didn't, much to her disappointment.

She wanted desperately to know what it felt like to have his hands on her, to be held by him, to feel his lips moving over hers. She wanted to touch him, to soothe away some of

CAMERON: THE SORORITY

the anger that always seemed to be simmering just beneath the surface, to run her fingers through his glossy black hair.

Later, she told herself, settling back into her seat as he pulled out of the parking lot.

Chapter 7

"How was your date with Tad?" Val asked, after knocking on Cameron's door first thing the next morning. "Did you have fun?"

Cameron rubbed her eyes and climbed back into her bed, yawning. "It was... does *perfect* say it all?"

Val smiled and sat on the desk chair opposite the bed. "It sure does. I'm really glad. He seemed like a nice guy."

"He is, but it goes way beyond that." Cameron leaned back on her pillow. Before Val's knock had wrenched her out of her pleasant dream, she'd been wrapped in Tad's arms, kissing him endlessly....

Only it wasn't a dream.

Okay, well, technically, it was a dream. But it was more like a recap of the end of their date the night before, when they'd come back up to her room and made out on her bed.

Cameron had known, when she'd invited him up, where it would lead, and she'd wondered if she was more anxious than he was. But she knew, the first time he kissed her—which was as soon as they'd closed the door behind them—that his passion matched her own, that he, too, had been waiting for this all night.

There had been nothing tentative about that first kiss. He'd taken her into his muscular arms the way she'd imagined, holding her against his hard chest as he brought his lips down over her own. He'd tasted and smelled like warm, fragrant chocolate—they'd gone out for hot-fudge sundaes after the movie—and his tongue had moved gently past her lips, sending quivers all over her.

She didn't remember how they'd gotten over to the bed. She only remembered lying there, with him on top of her, kissing endlessly, their hands roaming over each others' bodies, probing past clothing to stroke warm skin, until she'd realized that if she didn't stop him now, she wouldn't be able to stop herself.

And she didn't want to sleep with him, not on their first date. She was no virgin, thanks to a few serious boyfriends over the past couple of years, but she certainly wasn't the kind of girl who went this far with someone she really didn't know well.

And so she'd managed, somehow, to tear her lips from

Tad's, and to push him gently off of her and sit up. He'd understood, which was the incredible thing. He hadn't been grumpy about her putting the brakes on, and he hadn't tried to resume what they'd just been doing.

No, he'd smiled ruefully and said, "You're right. I'd better go."

He'd given her one last, sweet kiss at the door and then he was gone, leaving her to drift off to sleep on a pillow that was still warm and smelled like him.

"You should see your face," Val said, peering at her. "You're wearing this really sappy look, like Liesl in *The Sound of Music* movie when she sings 'Sixteen Going On Seventeen' with Rolf."

"I never saw *The Sound of Music*."

"You're kidding. I've seen it about a million times. On stage, too."

"So who's Liesl?"

"She's the oldest Von Trapp kid, and she's in love for the first time with this guy... only she doesn't know he's a Nazi."

"Oh." Cameron didn't want to think about Nazis. Not right now...

But it was too late. The mere mention promptly led her thoughts right back to the racism conversation she and Tad had had the night before.

It hadn't come up again after they'd gotten into the car. The movie they saw was a new Meg Ryan romantic comedy that left Cameron feeling great about herself, Tad, and the world

CAMERON: THE SORORITY

in general...not to mention anxious to be alone with Tad. It had banished all thoughts of their earlier conflict from her mind, and as they'd sat in the small, old-fashioned ice-cream shop afterward, their conversation had been light. She didn't remember exactly what they'd talked about, but it wasn't politics and it wasn't money—or the lack of it—and it wasn't sororities.

"What's wrong?" Val asked, still watching her.

"Nothing." She sat up. "How was the Omega party?"

"Very elegant. Very impressive. Very boring."

"You're kidding."

"Why are you surprised?"

"I wasn't. Couldn't you hear the sarcasm in my voice?"

Val smiled and shook her head. "It was so dull—a bunch of people standing in quiet little groups, trying to impress each other. But if you ask Lisa or Bethany, they'll probably say it was the best night of their lives. All the way home, all they talked about was how they can't wait to be Omegas."

"What about you? Are you still going to pledge them?"

"If I get a bid."

"You will. You're a legacy, remember?"

"Yeah, I remember."

They were both silent for a long time, and then, just as Cameron was going to ask Val what time she wanted to go to breakfast, the phone rang.

"Wow," she said with a laugh, getting out of bed. "I'm still not used to the luxury of having a phone in my room. Every time it rings, I jump."

"I do, too. But whenever ours rings, it's for Lisa." Val stood and walked to the door. "Knock when you're ready to go to the dining hall."

"I will," she said, lifting the receiver. "See you, Val. Hello?"

"Cam?"

She'd been half-expecting to hear Tad's voice, but she wasn't disappointed when she realized it was Allison.

"Hey, hi!"

"Who's Val?"

"She's a good friend of mine."

"The one from Long Island?"

"God, no! Val's the nice one. I think I told you about her. She's from Georgia."

"The rich one, right?" Allison asked.

"Down here, it seems like everyone's rich, Al. Well, almost everyone," she tacked on, thinking of Tad. "Hey, I had a date last night. My first one since I got here."

"See? I told you it wouldn't take you long. Me, I'll be lucky if anyone asks me out by the time I'm a senior. So who was he?"

"His name is Tad."

"Is *he* rich?"

"No. No way. He's actually the opposite. He's living at home with his parents and all these brothers and sisters. He was telling me about them last night."

"It's good to hear that people who live at home while they're in college can still get dates. Maybe all's not lost for me, after all."

Cameron smiled. "You'll be fine, Allison. College is great."

"Yeah, when you actually get to be a part of it. Somehow, I don't think you and I are going to have similar experiences, Cameron."

She couldn't argue there.

Poor Allison. It wouldn't even be so bad if her parents weren't so old-world Italian. Her father, who was nice enough but had hopelessly outdated ideas, ruled the house. Allison's curfew was ridiculously stringent, and she was always having to leave parties just when the fun was starting. She constantly had to call home to check in with her parents when she was out, and she was never able to relax, due to the constant fear that they'd decide to come out looking for her. They'd actually done it once, sophomore year—shown up at the Pines, which was a lakeside park with pavilions, and dragged Allison away from a party.

Cameron imagined the DeMitris pulling up to some fraternity party at State in their battered Chevy and hunting down their daughter. A wave of pity washed over her.

"Maybe you can move out next semester," Cameron suggested.

"Yeah, if I win the lottery."

Cameron changed the subject. "Hey, guess what? I got a letter from Zara the other day. It sounds like she's a little nervous about going away to school, huh?"

"Why? What did she say?"

"It wasn't anything specific. Just a feeling I got from her letter. How's she doing?"

"She *is* pretty worried—not that she says anything about it. But she's been even quieter than usual, and she doesn't seem excited about leaving next weekend. Unlike Kim, who's scheming ways to go early... which she can't do, because she can't get into her apartment until the first."

"What about Bridget?"

"Are you kidding? Do you think I've even seen her? She and Grant are spending every second together these days. It's like they're afraid they're never going to see each other again, or something. They're obsessed. I'm really worried about what she's going to do once she's so far away from him."

"Well, it's only for a semester, right?"

"That's the plan. But you don't know Mrs. Caddaham like I do. She's lost without her husband, and she's practically in bed all day, every day. I can't see how Grant's going to leave her, even in January."

"It's too bad he's an only child."

"The whole thing is too bad," Allison said. "I can't believe someone in his forties, this regular healthy guy, could just drop dead. I guess you never know. But let's not talk about such a depressing thing. Tell me about all the fun you're having with Rush."

"Actually, it's almost over. Bids come out right after classes start."

"Do you think you'll get one?"

"Not from the Omegas." She explained the situation to Allison.

"Well, was your date with this Tad guy worth it?"

"Definitely, definitely, definitely."

"So you did the right thing. Sounds like they're a bunch of stuck-up snobs, anyway. Are there other sororities you can join?"

"I really like the Lambdas," she said, ignoring the twinge of misgiving that poked up as she recalled what Tad had told her. "I was invited back to their dinner tonight. If they give me a bid, I'll be psyched."

"I hope it works out, Cameron. It sounds like you're making a lot of friends, though, so even if you don't get into a sorority, you'll probably have a blast."

She sounded so wistful.

Cameron said, "Yeah, I guess it'll be fine if I don't get in." There was no way she'd tell someone like Allison that if she had to go through college living in the dorms, not invited to any of the big Greek parties, she'd be miserable. Allison would kill for the chance to go away to a school like SFC, never mind pledging.

And anyway, Cameron knew that Tad would probably be thrilled if she didn't get a bid.

But what if she did? What if she pledged? How would he react then?

She tried to shove the thought out of her mind, but it kept trying to drift back in the whole time she was listening to Allison's account of the wild party Kim had thrown the night before at the Pines. According to Allison, it was even better than Kim's two-day graduation bash, which their newly liberated class had dubbed the Mother of all Parties.

As she hung up, Cameron thought that Weston Bay—and her friends—seemed farther away than ever.

She managed to escape a repeat of the other day's homesickness episode, though.

As she headed for the shower, she didn't let herself get into a melancholy mood. At least, not about that.

No, instead of thinking about her friends and family back home, wondering what she was missing, she worried about Tad and pledging and wondered why it suddenly seemed that one had to preclude the other.

He hadn't called by the time she had to leave for the Lambda dinner party, but he'd said he might not. He'd told her he was putting in a flagstone patio at a house in Lauderdale Lakes and wouldn't be back until early evening.

Cameron stayed in her room until the last possible second, dressed in her favorite outfit of all time—a black crepe designer dinner suit that made her look five inches taller and five pounds thinner.

At least, that was what Bethany had said when she'd seen her in it. She had a way of delivering insults in the form of compliments, Cameron had noticed. Whenever Bethany looked at her and opened her mouth to say something, Cameron braced herself.

Particularly now that she seemed to be having trouble fitting into her clothes as comfortably as she always had. The waistband on her skirt was tighter tonight than it had been when she'd tried it on a few days ago.

Of course, that might be due to the fact that she'd somehow eaten an entire bag of Doritos this afternoon. The giant size, Cool Ranch flavor. It was just sitting there in her room—a remnant from the snack binge she and Val had had one midnight—and so was she, waiting for the phone to ring. She'd thought that maybe Tad would get home earlier than he'd thought and call her.

She'd passed on going to the beach with the others, and instead sat on her bed, restlessly trying to read a Mary Higgins Clark suspense novel and listening to an old Lisa Loeb CD that reminded her of high school.

And gradually, the tortilla chips disappeared, until she found herself licking her finger to make sure she got every last crumb from the bottom of the bag. Disgusted, she'd realized she felt sick... and that she'd have to take another shower before tonight. She smelled like one big Mexican restaurant, and she knew brushing her teeth and washing her face wouldn't cut it.

At least taking a shower, doing her hair and makeup, and getting dressed gave her something constructive to do. But she was ready way too early, and then she was late meeting her friends in Bethany's room, much to the irritation of Lisa and Bethany. Even though they'd pretty much decided that they were going to get bids from the Omegas, they didn't want to be late to the dinner party.

Of course, Cameron didn't, either. The Lambdas were *it* for her. As the four of them headed up the walk at the Lambda house, which was softly lit with Frank Sinatra tunes spilling out into the warm evening air, she felt as though she were coming home.

That's such a corny thing to think, she told herself, climbing the front steps. *You really need to get out more. Spending the day alone with yourself is making you into a sap.*

The Lambdas had transformed the first floor of their house into what resembled a forties supper club—at least, that was what Val said. She watched a lot of old movies.

There were lots of little round tables, draped in soft pink cloths with lit oil lamps and fresh flowers in the center of each one. Tuxedoed waiters handed out flutes of champagne. The Lambdas were dressed elegantly, and they were gracious hostesses, leading their guests to their assigned tables and introducing them around.

Cameron found herself seated with another freshman hopeful, an amiable Texan named Kayla. She liked her instantly and learned that the Lambdas were Kayla's first choice in sororities, too.

"Don't ya just love this old house?" she kept saying, looking around with sparkly eyes. "Isn't this the *most* fun?"

Cameron felt the same way...until Randi showed up at their table. She was the only Lambda that Cameron had distinctly disliked at the New Year's party. It just figured that of all the sisters in the room, she was seated with Cameron.

She reminded her of Bethany, in a way, the way she went on and on about her summer back home in Chicago, where she lived on the North Shore. Her mother was a lawyer and her father was a doctor.

"Really? My father's a doctor, too," Cameron couldn't resist saying, but hated herself as soon as she did.

"What's his specialty?"

"He's a pediatrician."

"Oh. Mine is chief surgeon at Merciful Angels Hospital."

"That's nice," was all Cameron could think to say.

The other sister at their table, Leslie, was so quiet that Cameron couldn't get a handle on her personality. She might be nice, Cameron thought, when Leslie laughed pleasantly at one of Kayla's jokes. But then she caught her appraising the slightly gaudy ring Kayla was wearing, with her nose wrinkled ever so slightly, and Cameron wasn't so sure.

Dinner was incredible—lobster tail and a deliciously rich wild mushroom risotto that tasted as if it was loaded with butter. Dessert was chocolate-hazelnut torte served with hazelnut cream coffee. The china was antique Victorian, a pink floral pattern with delicate gold accents.

"Do you eat this way every night?" Kayla asked, pushing her empty torte plate away.

"Do you mean on the good china? One night a week, we do, with candlelight and all that jazz," Randi said.

"No, I meant the food. If I lived here, I'd blow up and weigh two hundred pounds," Kayla told them, giggling.

COLLEGE LIFE 101

"So would I," Cameron put in, wishing she could unfasten the top button on her waistband.

"Well, we don't always have lobster and champagne, but the food *is* wonderful—well, most of it," Randi amended. "Some people have rather...strange taste in food."

"What do you mean?" asked Kayla.

"There's one girl who loves collard greens and black-eyed peas. And she's no nigger, either," she added with a laugh. "I can't figure it out."

The creamy torte on Cameron's tongue turned instantly to a mass of vile sludge, and she had to gulp water from her crystal goblet to get it down. Her hands were trembling and her face suddenly felt as if it had a flaming sunburn.

Around her, Randi, Leslie and Kayla were going on with their conversation as if nothing had happened. The other two hadn't blinked an eye at the racial slur that had rolled so casually off Randi's tongue.

It's not that big a deal, Cameron tried telling herself, fighting the sickening feeling in her stomach. *Just calm down.*

But it was a big deal. These girls had no idea that Cameron's father—her father the *doctor*—was a *nigger*. They didn't know that her beloved Grandma Elma was a *nigger*...that Cameron *herself* was a *nigger*.

"Are you all right?" Kayla was asking, looking at her strangely.

"What? Oh..." Cameron realized that the three of them were looking at her, and that she'd pushed back her chair and was clenching the edge of the table so tightly her hands ached.

"I need to use the ladies' room," she managed to get out before she stood and hurried away.

Upstairs, alone in the first bathroom she found, she locked the door and let out a deep breath.

Nigger.

It was such an ugly word, such a hateful word.

Her eyes filled with tears and then, without warning, a wave of nausea washed over her, sending her to the toilet. She threw up, all of it, the torte and the lobster and the risotto, and the Cool Ranch Doritos, too. The champagne had turned to acid, choking her as she heaved.

And even when her stomach was empty she retched over the bowl, consumed by shuddering dry heaves, as if her body wanted to expel the rest of it, too. All the anger and confusion and disbelief that had come to a head at the sound of that one nasty word.

Finally she managed to stand and flush, and to move shakily back to the sink, where she stared at herself in the mirror. She was expecting to see a nightmarish distortion of herself.

To her astonishment, she looked fine.

Her makeup—save her lipstick—was intact, her hair still held back in the rhinestone clip, falling softly past her shoulders.

The only thing that had changed since she'd looked in the mirror right before she left her room was her eyes. Earlier she had seen happy anticipation in them. Now they were filled with a haunted expression.

She couldn't banish it before she left the bathroom, and it

was still there when she got back to the dorm late that night.

As she stood before the mirror in her room, removing her makeup, she thought about what had happened.

Randi's comment had effectively ruined her evening, and so much more than that.

She didn't know if she wanted to be a Lambda anymore—not after what Tad had told her, and now this.

If she did pledge, what would they do when they found out about Cameron's background? Would they kick her out?

They can't do that, she told herself firmly. *That would be... it would be...*

She thought again of the lone black girl at the Omega tea. She knew that girl hadn't been invited back, that she wouldn't be asked to pledge. Not the Omegas. And not the Lambdas, either, because she hadn't been in attendance at tonight's dinner.

Maybe no sorority would consider her. Maybe there was an unwritten rule at SFC; maybe Cameron was the only one who wasn't aware of it.

Fury boiled up inside her, and she bit her lower lip so hard she saw herself wince in the mirror.

She put the makeup remover aside and turned away, unable to look at herself any longer. She just wanted to go to sleep, so that she could shut it all out.

She climbed into bed and turned out the light, even though it was just a few minutes past ten. She hadn't been in bed before two since she'd arrived at school.

CAMERON: THE SORORITY

Her friends had gone out for coffee after the party, but she'd told them she wasn't feeling well. The last thing she wanted to do was rehash the evening... or face the concerned look on Val's face.

It was obvious she knew something was wrong with Cameron. After dinner, when they were seated in the parlor and the Lambdas were serenading them with their sorority song, Val had asked in a whisper if Cameron was all right. And she hadn't seemed satisfied with Cameron's nod and attempt at a reassuring smile.

When the phone rang at ten-thirty, Cameron was still awake, lying in the dark, her body tense and her fists clenched at her side.

It might be Tad.

Or it could be Valerie.

Or maybe even her mother, who had known tonight was the big occasion of the Lambda dinner.

She let it ring.

Cameron woke to the sound of a key turning in the door. Panic washed over her as she sat up, bleary-eyed and confused.

"Hello?" a female stranger called as the door started to open.

"Who is it?" Cameron's voice came out in a croak.

"It's me, your roommate."

She blinked and saw an unfamiliar girl standing in the doorway, an enormous satchel slung over her shoulder. She was dark-skinned with aquiline features and large black eyes beneath slightly hooded lids. Her ebony hair was short and glossy, her frame slight.

Cameron heard a gasp and thought it had come from herself until she noted the expression on the girl's face. She looked... well, horrified.

Following the direction of her roommate's gaze, she saw the rumpled black crepe outfit, stockings, shoes, and all, lying directly in front of the door, where Cameron had stripped it off the moment she came in last night.

Then there were the piles of clothes—some folded, some wadded into balls—all over the bare mattress of the other bed. The crumpled Doritos bag, along with assorted other empty packages and cans, were strewn around an overflowing wastebasket. Cameron's trunk sat in the middle of the floor, clothes spilling out of it and draped over the lid.

Oh, God.

"You must be Sharma," Cameron said, struggling to sound welcoming. "I'm Cameron Collier."

"It's Shanta," came the reply, in a tone she couldn't read. "Shanta Sahir."

"Nice to meet you. I didn't know you were coming this morning..."

"Obviously."

Amazingly, the comment wasn't laced with sarcasm. Nor was Shanta's next remark.

"And actually, it isn't morning. It's afternoon."

"It is?" Cameron glanced at the digital clock near her bed and saw that it was nearly one o'clock. How had she slept so long? Why hadn't Val come by to go to breakfast?

Then she vaguely remembered hearing someone knock on her door in the middle of the night. At least, she'd *thought* it was the middle of the night. She'd ignored it, slipping easily back into the comforting, numbing dream she'd been having.

What was it about?

For a moment, she couldn't recall. Then bits and pieces came drifting back to her, in that fragmented habit dreams had. She'd been at home—her mother was stroking her head and asking her if she wanted some hot tea. And her father was there, laughing his booming laugh and tossing her up into the air the way he used to do when she was younger. She'd felt happy, and carefree, and secure...

Until now.

Now it was back to reality with a bang, back to this disaster area of a room and the stranger who still stood in the doorway, uncertainty having settled in over her exotic features.

Cameron sat up and swung her feet over the edge of the bed. "Come on in," she invited, rubbing her eyes.

"Actually, that's all right. Maybe I'll just leave my bag here and...and come back later. My parents are downstairs in the car with the rest of my stuff. They want to go to lunch...we'll go to lunch, and we'll come back in an hour. Or two."

Cameron was nodding, and so was the girl. An unspoken

message crossed between them. When Shanta came back in a few hours, the room would be clean.

As soon as the door had closed behind her new roommate, Cameron let out her breath. She hadn't even realized she'd been holding it.

At least the girl hadn't freaked out on her, or been nasty about the shambles that had greeted her.

It would have helped if she'd at least given Cameron some advance warning that she was arriving today, though. Or the school could have...

Her eye fell on a sheet of folded stationery she'd stuck into the edge of the mirror between the closets. She knew exactly what it was. The letter Shanta had sent her just a few days ago, introducing herself and saying that she'd be arriving on Saturday.

Was today Saturday?

Obviously, you ditz, Cameron thought, still too groggy to move. She hadn't been keeping track of days very well... but then, life had lost its sense of routine ever since she'd arrived at SFC. And she'd been blithely carried along with the whirlwind of parties, and new friends, and the dorm, and Tad...

Suddenly she wanted no part of any of that.

And she sure as hell didn't feel like having her privacy invaded by a total stranger.

It figured that just when she desperately needed space, she no longer had it. In just two hours there would be no place where Cameron could lock herself away, to be alone with her thoughts.

I have to escape, she thought, suddenly overcome by a feeling of claustrophobia. *I can't deal with this now. I can't stay here.*

Not that she had any choice.

She *had* to stay.

Where else was there to go?

An idea popped into her head, an idea that was so crazy and irrational that it might as well have been launched from way out in space.

How on earth did you come up with that? Cameron wondered, shaking her head and frowning.

It was ridiculous.

It was impossible.

It was also her only option.

Before she could stop to reconsider, she was up and across the room, lifting the receiver and dialing.

"Yes, please," she heard herself saying as she fumbled for a pen and a scrap of paper to write on. "I'd like the number for Mrs. Myra Bainbridge in Boca Raton."

Chapter 8

Vista Cove, the retirement condo community where her grandmother lived, was ten miles from the bus stop. Since her grandmother hadn't offered to pick her up, Cameron got into a cab, trying not to be disconcerted by the middle-aged driver's unbearable B.O. Opening both back windows helped.

"I have air conditioning on," he kept saying in broken English.

She nodded and smiled, as if she didn't understand, and she kept the windows down.

As the cab drove along a wide, palm-tree-lined boulevard, Cameron thought about the phone conversation she'd had with her grandmother earlier.

Myra Bainbridge had clearly been surprised to hear from

her... maybe not pleasantly surprised, but not exactly dispassionate, either.

"Cameron, how are you, dear?" she'd asked a bit hesitantly, in that formal way of hers.

"I'm fine, Grandma. I'm here in Florida—"

"Tallahassee, isn't it?"

"No, actually, I'm outside Fort Lauderdale."

"That's nice. Then you're near the ocean. And are you enjoying college?"

"Well, classes haven't started yet," she'd said. "I thought I might come up and visit you in Boca...."

She'd trailed off, waiting for her grandmother's reaction.

"That would be nice, Cameron," Myra said graciously. "In a few weeks when you're settled—"

"Actually, I was thinking of today."

Pause.

Cameron was about to open her mouth and say something, *anything*, to diffuse the awkward silence.

But then her grandmother had said, "You want to come *today*? But how would you get here? I still have the Cadillac," she added hastily, "but I don't care for highway driving, and Fort Lauderdale is much too big a trip anyway."

"I can take a bus," Cameron offered, thinking *please, please let me come*. "I can spend the night... if you have room."

"Well, there's the pull-out couch—" Her grandmother sounded slightly flustered. "And I do have a bridge luncheon tomorrow, but it isn't until noon. I suppose if you don't mind taking the bus—I don't even know how to find out the schedule—"

"I can take care of that," Cameron had assured her, as relief washed over her. "I just need your address. I'll get there."

And so, here she was, seated in the back of this smelly rattle-trap cab, driving past two white stone pillars and a sign that said, *Welcome to Vista Cove.*

They had to stop at a little guardhouse and give her grandmother's name, then wait while the security man buzzed Myra on the phone. Then they were given clearance, along with finger-pointing directions. The cab proceeded along a wide, winding lane bordered by lush tropical foliage, past rows of identical white stucco buildings with terra cotta roofs.

Finally the driver stopped in front of one of them and looked over his shoulder at Cameron.

"This is it?" she asked, thinking that her grandmother was probably waiting outside for her. But Myra Bainbridge was nowhere in sight.

Cameron paid the driver and grabbed her bag. She headed up the tile walkway, up a flight of steps, and knocked on the door marked 25-K-B.

"Cameron, is that you?"

"Yup."

Who else would it be? she wanted to ask, thinking that the security guard had just alerted her grandmother that she was on her way over.

There was the sound of locks clicking, and then the door

was thrown open and Myra Bainbridge was standing there.

She looks so much older, Cameron thought, staring at the white-haired woman whose pale skin resembled the papery outer layer of a garlic bulb. She wore glasses and a light green pants suit with low heels, and she smelled of some powdery perfume.

"Hello, dear," she said, and leaned forward for an awkward hug.

"Hi, Grandma. Thank you so much for having me over."

"Come right in. How was your trip?" Her southern accent wasn't nearly as pronounced as Lisa's or Mary Jo's. "Was the bus crowded?"

"Actually, it was almost empty," she said, thinking that she was the only one foolish enough to take local service up the coast on a beautiful Saturday afternoon when everyone else in the world was at the beach.

That was where her friends back at the dorm had been headed. Val had stopped by just as Cameron was coming out of the shower, and had stuck around long enough to help her throw all her clutter into her closet and trunk and jam them closed. The stuff that wouldn't fit went under Cameron's bed, tossed haphazardly.

At least the place looked presentable for Shanta.

And at least Cameron had someplace to go so that she wouldn't have to listen to Val's well-meaning questions about whether she was all right—and she wouldn't have to answer the phone, which had rung several times.

It was probably Tad, she'd thought, or maybe it wasn't—maybe he didn't plan on calling her anymore. Their date the other night suddenly seemed like ages ago. She didn't have the energy to worry about a relationship. She didn't even have the energy to talk to her friends or have fun. All she wanted was a reprieve—and it looked like she had one.

Apartment 25-K-B in Vista Cove was about as far as you could get from Thayer Hall.

Her grandmother's apartment was spotless, for one thing. It smelled of pine disinfectant and lemon furniture polish, though there was a strong hint of stale cigarette smoke permeating the rooms, as though it had been months since fresh air had blown through.

The magazines on the glass coffee table were spread in a perfect fan, the round wooden coasters precisely stacked beside them. And though there were several houseplants, there wasn't a shriveled leaf or speck of potting soil in evidence. No dust, no cobwebs, no clutter.

And everything was so...white. The carpet, the walls, the furniture. Cameron felt as though she was leaving smudges everywhere she went—in the bathroom, where she freshened up, and in the small spare bedroom, where she stashed her overnight bag in a closet because it seemed so reckless to toss it on the uncomfortable-looking couch.

Cameron paused in the hallway outside the guest room to examine a large framed portrait that hung on the wall. It was a formal, posed photograph, with her grandmother seated and her grandfather standing behind her, his hand on her shoulder. Cameron figured it must have been taken a good ten years ago.

The wall around the portrait was dotted with other, smaller framed photos. Some were black and whites of her grandparents in their youth, and there were several of Cameron's mother at various stages over the years. The last was her college graduation portrait—Cameron recognized that one; her father had a copy of it on his desk in his office back home, along with their wedding portrait.

It struck her then that her grandmother didn't have a picture from the Colliers' wedding day—nor any of Cameron or her sisters. Or, if she did, none were displayed on the wall.

Cameron frowned. She was certain her mother had sent the Bainbridges photographs over the years. In fact, she remembered impatiently Christmas shopping with her mother, who was seeking the perfect frame to hold a family portrait she was sending her parents. The frame had to be light-colored wood, with a pastel-colored mat to match the Bainbridges' decor.

It had been Cameron who finally located just the right frame, way at the bottom of a stack, and her mother had been so grateful she'd splurged on a new sweater for Cameron afterward. She still had it, a navy cashmere crewneck.

But apparently, her grandmother no longer had the frame or the portrait. Or if she did, it wasn't on display.

So what? Cameron thought. *Maybe she lost it.*

But how did you lose a sixteen-by-twenty family portrait?

She met her grandmother back in the kitchen, where Myra was standing at the counter smoking a just-lit cigarette.

"Here's your iced tea," Myra said, pushing a glass toward her. "I just made it, so it might not be cold yet, and I'm afraid I don't have any ice. But there's lemon..."

"It's all right," Cameron said, taking a sip.

Actually, it wasn't all right. Far from it. The stuff was lukewarm and had the dank smell of Florida tapwater. There were clumps of mix, and it wasn't even the presweetened kind, but the nasty, slightly acidic stuff you sometimes got when you ordered an iced tea at a fast-food restaurant.

She forced down a swallow and realized, as it sloshed into her empty stomach, that she hadn't eaten since she'd been sick last night. She was positively hollow. There hadn't even been time to grab a candy bar before she'd run to catch the bus outside the student union.

"Are you hungry?" her grandmother asked, as if she'd read her mind.

"Actually, I am." Cameron sat gingerly—and expectantly—on a stool at a white-tile topped breakfast bar.

Was her grandmother going to whip up some good old-fashioned homemade comfort food? Her mouth watered as Cameron thought of Grandma Elma's famous baked mashed potatoes with sour cream and chives. She was always telling Cameron that you couldn't deal with problems on an empty stomach.

Maybe her grandmother Bainbridge had the same philosophy. Maybe she'd start chopping onions and opening cans, and listen sympathetically to Cameron's tales of woe while she cooked.

"Would you like a banana?"

"Pardon?" Cameron blinked.

"A banana? There's just one left. It's a bit overripe, I'm afraid...." Her grandmother had set her cigarette down in an ashtray and was wielding what resembled a wizened black boomerang. "Or I could make you some toast."

"Uh..." Cameron glanced at the clock. It was five-forty-two. Time for supper. "Why don't we go out to eat? My treat," she added, to sweeten the pot.

"Oh, dear, I've already been out to eat. Millie and I went to the early-bird special down at Marino's hours ago. I assumed you would already have had dinner, since you were arriving so late...."

"It's all right," Cameron said, suddenly feeling incredibly cranky. Must be the low blood sugar. "Maybe...I'll have toast."

"All right." Her grandmother started for the bread box on the pristine countertop. "I might have a can of soup, too...."

"That would be good."

Right now a hunk of shoe leather would be good.

"Cream of celery," her grandmother said, surveying the contents of the cupboard. "And chicken consommé."

"Oh..."

"Which do you prefer?"

"I—I'll just stick with the toast, thanks. That's fine."

"All right." As if relieved, her grandmother turned toward the toaster and fed two slices of what looked like whole-wheat bread into the top. She pushed down the lever, then glanced back at Cameron. "How's your mother?"

"My mother?" Cameron shrugged. "She's great. She has a photo spread in *December Bride* this month."

"*December Bride*?"

"It's this new magazine for old—uh, older women. You know, older women who are getting married again."

"I see. And how are your sisters?"

"They're fine. Oh, I mean, I guess Hayley has the flu or something, but other than that... everyone's fine. Dad went to some conference in New York before I left."

"Oh? That's nice. What kind of conference?" her grandmother asked in one of those this-is-so-boring-and-I-couldn't-care-less tones.

"It was for some African-American medical association."

"I see." Her grandmother inspected the toaster.

Was it Cameron's imagination, or did she look uncomfortable?

Be real. Have you ever seen this woman look comfortable? she asked herself.

The answer was no, of course. Her grandmother always seemed to be adhering to some preordained code of manners.

"Here you go," she said, setting the toast on a plain white plate in front of Cameron. "I don't have any jelly, but there's honey...."

CAMERON: THE SORORITY

She trailed off expectantly with her hand on the cupboard door, almost as if she thought Cameron would tell her not to bother.

"Thanks, honey would be good," Cameron said, surveying the two small pieces of toast before her. She wondered if it would be rude to ask for two more pieces, and decided that it would. At least, in this particular place under these particular circumstances.

"Do you enjoy school? What are you taking?" her grandmother asked, taking a drag of her cigarette as Cameron spread a generous dollop of honey on each slice.

"Classes haven't started yet, but I'm already registered, so I know my schedule. Just the usual Freshman stuff. A history course and an English Comp and Intro to Soc."

"Soc?"

"Sociology. It's supposed to be an interesting class."

"That's nice." Again, her grandmother was wearing that polite but detached expression.

"So what have you been up to?" Cameron asked, thinking it would be nice to find out what her grandmother's life was all about.

Myra Bainbridge looked pleased at her interest. "Oh, not much at all these days" was her reply. "I've mostly been helping Millie sort through her husband's things—"

"Who's Millie? Sorry, I didn't mean to interrupt."

Her grandmother smiled tightly. "Millie's my next door neighbor. She usually comes over for Sanka and television on

Saturday nights. We like to watch game shows."

"Sounds fun," Cameron said, wondering what she was doing here. Sanka and game shows. Great. "What time is Millie coming?"

"She isn't, this evening. I told her I was unexpectedly having company, so..."

"It's all right," Cameron said, feeling awkward. "I mean, she can come if she wants. I won't, um, mind or anything, if that's what you're—"

"No, Millie won't be coming over. She's very understanding. Anyway"—her grandmother cleared her throat and went on, as though she'd been in the middle of a conversation about something else—"Millie's husband, Roger, died last spring."

"That's too bad."

"It is. He was a nice man. Millie's going through his closets and drawers, you know, gathering things for the autumn clothing drive at our church."

Cameron had nothing to say to that, so she smiled and nodded as though she were interested.

Her grandmother talked a bit more, about Millie's divorced daughter who lived in Minneapolis and how it was a shame she couldn't find time to fly down to help her mother. And about how Millie had just had gall bladder surgery, poor thing.

Cameron's thoughts wandered to Tad. Had he tried to call her? Was he wondering where she'd disappeared to?

Val was the only person who knew where she'd gone. And all she knew was that Cameron was visiting her grandmother in Boca. She'd looked at Cameron somewhat oddly when she'd told her that, and Cameron realized that until now Val hadn't even known she *had* a grandmother in Boca. Maybe she thought Cameron was lying, that she wanted to keep her real destination secret.

But Val wasn't the type to ask too many questions or push an issue. She'd simply told Cameron to have a good time and be careful.

Well, you can't be any more careful than this, Cameron thought. *I can't believe I'm in the middle of a retirement community eating whole wheat toast and discussing Millie's gall bladder.*

Last night's bitter disappointment had ebbed, and Cameron realized it probably hadn't been necessary to flee up the coast to a grandmother who might as well be a stranger. In fact, she would probably have been better off back at school. She could have gone to the beach with the others, or even taken the bus over to Sawgrass Mills to go shopping.

But then, there was the roommate situation. She was used to having privacy. Shanta was probably a nice person and Cameron would probably quickly grow accustomed to sharing the room, but today just wasn't the right time to start a new relationship—especially one that would have to be forged under such close quarters.

So instead you took a rattly bus for nearly two hours to jumpstart a relationship with a grandmother you've barely seen. Brilliant.

And now she was going to have to deal with her mother,

who was bound to find it unsettling that Cameron had this sudden interest in her grandmother after all these years. Why that should be unsettling, Cameron didn't know... but she figured that was how her mother would feel.

Unless she was wrong.

Maybe Shelley Collier would be glad that Cameron had looked up her mother, gone to visit her. Maybe she'd say it was about time someone took steps to mend the fences....

If they truly needed mending.

Cameron wondered, as she watched her grandmother light another cigarette, why she hadn't been a part of the Colliers' lives. Whose choice had it been?

Or was it simply time and distance that had kept them apart for most of Cameron's eighteen years?

She had thought this visit with Myra Bainbridge might shed some light on the situation, but she realized she was wrong. Her grandmother wasn't going to open up to her. She wasn't the emotional type; that much was clear. Cameron sensed that if she started asking personal questions, her grandmother would shut her out completely... or maybe even get angry. Even ask her to leave.

The woman was distinctly nervous over her being here. She wasn't exactly relaxing or warming up as the minutes passed, either.

Cameron regretted her impulsive decision to visit, but it was too late now. She was stuck spending the night with a stranger—a stranger who was her own flesh and blood, but who hardly acted that way.

Something... there must be something in the past that caused the rift between her and Mom, Cameron thought.

And she was suddenly too weary—and too afraid of the truth—to consider the possible things that may have gone wrong.

The first person Cameron saw when she arrived back at Thayer on Sunday afternoon was Val. Her friend was just coming out the front door as Cameron inserted her magnetic card to unlock it.

"Hey!" they said in unison.

"You just getting back?" Val asked.

"Yup. Where are you going?"

"I have to go buy some Advil."

"Wicked night of partying?"

"I wish," Val said, shaking her head. "Actually, it's my tooth. It's killing me. I lost a filling last night eating a candy apple."

"Where'd you eat a candy apple?"

"At the Alpha carnival," Val said with a shrug.

"Hey, how was that?"

"It was fun," her friend said simply.

Cameron knew Val wasn't the type to gush about a party, particularly one that had excluded Cameron from the guest list. She also knew Val had no intention of joining the Alphas. But their carnival night was rumored to be one of the best rush parties on campus. It had to have been a lot more than *fun.*

"Listen, Cameron," Val said, "I met your new roommate last night. I invited her to join us for dinner."

"Did she?"

"Yeah. She's sweet."

"That's good. I bet she was relieved to have the place to herself for her first twenty-four hours on campus. Did she say anything about how I cleaned it up?"

"No, nothing about that. But she did ask me who Tad was."

Cameron's stomach transformed itself into a high-flying acrobat. "Why did she ask that?"

"Because I guess he called you a few times yesterday. Shanta didn't know where you were. She asked me, and I didn't know what to tell her. I didn't know if you'd want Tad to find out about your visit with your grandmother."

The way she said it made Cameron think Val didn't believe that was where she'd really been.

"Look, Val, I was up in Boca at this crazy retirement condo with my grandmother. I swear..."

"I didn't say you weren't."

"But I can tell by the look on your face that you think I was actually out... what? Scoring some crack? Hooking in the red light district?"

Val laughed, and so did Cameron.

"I didn't even know you *had* a grandmother in Boca," she said. "Is this the one who doesn't get along with your mother?"

"This is the one."

"Did you have a nice time with her?"

"'Nice' doesn't exactly cover it. We watched game shows and drank Sanka and this morning we went to breakfast at some pancake house at, like, *dawn*. I had been starving all night, but I couldn't even look at food that early in the day. And then we went to church...which was like this major Holy Roller experience, believe me."

"I believe you."

"I never knew my grandmother was so into religion. But then, I never knew my grandmother, period," she added.

"Then it was probably a good thing to spend some time with her, huh?"

"I guess. Tell me about Tad," she said anxiously.

"I don't know what's up with him. Only that he kept calling you yesterday."

"How about today?"

"I have no idea. But I think Shanta was going to the library for the day, so she probably wasn't there to pick up the phone if he called."

"The library? Classes haven't even started yet!"

"Shanta's very intelligent," Val told her. "She's...very serious about school."

"Why does it sound like you're warning me?"

"I'm not. Not exactly. I just wanted you to be aware that your roommate probably won't be thrilled if we have wee-hour burrito fests in your room."

Cameron sighed. "And I guess she wouldn't be thrilled to have Tad spend the night, either, huh?"

"Has he?"

"No! Not yet, anyway. But that doesn't mean that down the road…"

"Say no more. Listen, why don't you dump your bag and come with me to the drugstore?"

Cameron contemplated that, then shook her head. "I would, but I want to go up and see if I can get a hold of Tad. Maybe he left a number."

"You didn't have his number?"

"No. He lives at home with his family. He didn't offer to give it to me, and I didn't ask. But now I wish I had. I suddenly can't wait to talk to him."

"You know, I figured something had gone wrong between you two, the way you took off yesterday," Val said. "I didn't realize you were still interested."

"I'm definitely still interested," Cameron said, nodding. "*Very* interested. I just… got sidetracked. By a lot of stuff that totally doesn't matter."

And that, she decided, was the truth. She'd gotten herself all worked up over nothing. One racist comment… so what?

There was no reason to tell Tad what Randi had said. She had no desire to throw more fuel on the fire where he and the sorority issue were concerned.

And there was no reason to think that if she pledged the Lambdas, she could no longer date Tad.

Or that if she dated Tad, she couldn't pledge the Lambdas. So her life wasn't a disaster after all.

In fact, she thought as she took the stairs two at a time, things were definitely looking up.

Chapter 9

"**Another** sorority party?" Shanta asked, looking up from the thick textbook she was marking with a fluorescent orange highlighter.

"No, not a party. Actually, I have a date tonight," Cameron said, surveying her reflection in the mirror.

She decided her pants would look better with a shirt hanging out over them—her stomach wasn't as flat as it used to be. She definitely had to start doing sit-ups.

Tomorrow, she promised herself. *I'll do fifty sit-ups first thing when I wake up.*

Shanta was still watching her, the highlighter poised over a page. She wore reading glasses and was dressed in navy sweatpants and a matching sweatshirt, and her hair was tousled—

not that she seemed to mind. Cameron had already concluded that Shanta wasn't a girl who worried much about her looks.

This was one of the first times the two of them had been in the room together, awake, since Shanta had arrived. She spent most of her time in the library—which was beyond Cameron, who couldn't imagine what would happen when classes actually started.

And Shanta invariably came straight back to the room after dinner, in bed with the lights out before ten o'clock every night.

Cameron had invited her to the movies with her and Val last night, but she'd turned down the invitation politely, saying she was tired.

Cameron had wanted to tell her that if she didn't get up each morning before six—and for no conceivable reason, since she just hung around, reading before breakfast—she wouldn't be so exhausted. It wasn't as if she were reading anything interesting, even. Just dull, thick textbooks. Even Zara didn't read textbooks in her free time.

"Are you going out with Tad?" Shanta asked, apparently in a chatty mood.

"Yup." Cameron smiled at her reflection and saw a poppy seed trapped between her teeth. Oh, gross. She nabbed it with her pinky nail.

"Tad's your boyfriend, right?"

"Not exactly. We've only gone out once. We've been trying to hook up the past three days, but he's been busy working, and the few hours he's had free, I've been at Rush parties."

Shanta nodded. "Rush is almost over, though, isn't it?"

"It is over. Now we have to wait for the bids to come in. But that won't happen for a few more days."

"You're sure you want to join a sorority?"

"I'm positive... *if* I get asked." She crossed her fingers and showed Shanta, who frowned slightly.

"It doesn't bother you that these groups are elitist?"

"What do you mean by that?" Cameron uncrossed her fingers and tried to ignore the little *thud* in her stomach.

"They don't allow most people to join. They arbitrarily select—and exclude. And I've heard that membership is often based on things like how much money a person has, or what she looks like, or what race—"

"I don't think that's true," Cameron said quickly, not meeting Shanta's gaze. "Good grades count a lot. And what kind of civic stuff you did in high school—like, if you played bingo with the old folks every Saturday, or served Christmas dinner at the homeless shelter, they're interested in you. Most of the sororities have philanthropic causes."

"That's good." Shanta nodded. "I didn't realize that. So that's why you're so anxious to join?"

No. I mainly want to join because they have wild parties and I'll make a lot of friends and meet a ton of guys. What can I say? Maybe I'm just a shallow person.

"Yeah, that's basically it," Cameron said aloud. "How about you? Have you considered joining a sorority?"

"Oh, no," Shanta said quickly. "I would never have time for such..."

CAMERON: THE SORORITY   173

She trailed off, and Cameron wondered, *Such what? Nonsense? Foolishness?*

It was clear from her tone that Shanta considered sororities a waste of time, but Cameron didn't push the issue. She wasn't in the mood to get caught up in anything stressful.

Not right now. Not when she was due to meet Tad out front any second.

He'd told her to be waiting on the steps of Thayer, and he'd swing by and pick her up in his car. That way he wouldn't have to park way out in the commuter lot.

Cameron wasn't an old-fashioned kind of girl who expected her dates to knock on her door and escort her to their cars, but she had been a bit surprised at Tad's suggestion. He was the one who had seemed a little old-fashioned—on their first date, he'd held all the doors for her and pulled out her chairs and insisted on paying for everything. So it seemed odd that he didn't plan to park and come in.

"I have to get moving," she told Shanta, grabbing her purse. "If my mom calls, tell her I'll catch her first thing in the morning."

"You're expecting a call from her?"

"She *better* get in touch. She's supposed to be finding out what happened to my other trunk," Cameron said, frowning.

"What other trunk?"

Oh, great. Now wasn't a good time to break the news to her roommate. Especially when Cameron had finally managed to get her side of the room organized without infringing too much on Shanta's space. The only thing that crossed the unofficial boundary was the trunk, which she'd set up as sort of a bench. Val had surprised her with a gift of Laura Ashley throw pillows to scatter on top, and it looked like a cozy little seat—not that anyone ever sat there yet.

But we definitely could, Cameron reminded herself, and felt a little better.

"Cameron? What other trunk?" Shanta repeated, looking a little edgy.

"I, uh, had another one that was being shipped from home," Cameron explained quickly. "It never arrived, so we put a tracer on it. I'm really upset because all my stuff is inside."

"All your stuff?" Shanta echoed.

"Well, all my *important* stuff. Like family photos, that sort of thing." Her gaze wandered to Shanta's dressertop, where framed pictures of her parents and younger brother were arranged carefully. In one formal shot Mr. and Mrs. Sahir were dressed in traditional Indian garb—he in a turban, she in a sari.

When Lisa had spotted the photo the other day, she'd grabbed it and giggled. "Look, it's Gandhi," she'd exclaimed. "And Mrs. Gandhi. What's up with the red dot on this lady's head? Does she have one measle, or what?"

Cameron had said nothing, grateful that Shanta was safely in the library and hadn't overheard Lisa's comment.

She'd wondered what Lisa would think if she saw the picture her own mother had taken of her father a few years ago at a Kwanza celebration, wearing customary African clothing.

CAMERON: THE SORORITY

That particular photo was safely tucked away back home in her mother's portfolio, so there was no chance of anyone teasing her about it—or worse.

"What do you think happened to your trunk?" Shanta was asking her now. "Is it lost for good?"

"God, I hope not," Cameron said, thinking that Shanta was probably thinking the opposite. "Don't worry," she added hastily, "when it does come, it's not going to take up much space. And I'm trying to arrange to have it stored someplace else."

She made a mental note to do that. She'd just been so busy with other things until now.

"It's okay," Shanta said. "We'll find room for it if you can't. I'll bet we can squeeze it in somehow."

Cameron smiled gratefully.

Until now, she had been wishing that her roommate could have been a bit more like *her*—less studious, more social. Someone who could become a good friend, as Val had. But that suddenly didn't seem to matter as much. She was lucky, she knew, that Shanta was considerate and tolerant.

She vowed to be less sloppy and to spend more time talking to her roommate. Until now, she'd just sort of skimmed past her. But Shanta was sort of intriguing, and she seemed genuinely interested in what Cameron was doing.

"Well, I'd better get going," Cameron said, checking her watch and heading for the door. "Have a good night."

"You, too. Have fun on your date."

"I will." She hesitated in the doorway, then spontaneously

said, "You know, maybe sometime Tad could find a friend for you and we could double date."

As soon as she'd said it, she wanted to take it back. What on earth had possessed her to say such a crazy thing?

The look on Shanta's face was so taken aback, so genuinely surprised. Belatedly, she realized she'd implied that Shanta couldn't find a date on her own.

"I didn't mean—"

"It's nice of you to offer," Shanta cut in gently, "but I can't date."

"You can't date? Why not?" Probably because her parents wouldn't let her.

I'll have to fill Allison in on this one, Cameron thought. *She thinks her parents are ridiculous.*

"Because I'm engaged."

Cameron didn't think she'd heard her right. "Excuse me?"

"I'm engaged. To Mohan," she added, gesturing at one of the framed photos on her dresser. It showed a dark-skinned young man with big, solemn black eyes. He was casually dressed in jeans and a T-shirt and staring at the camera.

"But I...I thought that was your brother. He looks so much like you."

"He's actually related to me, distantly."

Cameron tried not to look too startled. Her thoughts were spinning. "How...how did you meet him?"

"I never have. He lives in New Delhi."

"India?" Cameron asked stupidly.

Shanta only nodded. "It's an arranged marriage. I know it sounds strange to you, but it's part of our culture.... My parents and his parents arranged it when we were both thirteen. I'm going to meet him this winter."

"So you don't... you don't love him?"

"I'm sure I'll learn to." Shanta's tone was matter-of-fact. "Statistically, arranged marriages in my country have a higher success rate than regular marriages here in America."

Cameron was speechless, not just at the facts Shanta was quoting, but at her roommate's bizarre circumstances. She couldn't imagine being engaged at this age, let alone to someone she'd never even met.

But she struggled to act as though she were taking the situation in stride, not wanting to offend Shanta. "Your fiancé is really handsome, Shanta. You must be excited about planning your wedding."

Shanta shrugged. "I'm more excited about school. I've always wanted to study law."

"That's why you're always reading and studying? You're going to become a lawyer?"

"Hopefully. It's been my fondest dream since I was a little girl."

Cameron saw the sparkle in Shanta's eyes and wondered what it would be like to have such passion for something. She thought about how enthusiastically Tad had spoken about politics, and how Val wanted to become a teacher.

What if she went through four years of school and never

figured out what she wanted to do with her life? Shanta already had a fiancé lined up, and a career. She seemed to know exactly where she was headed.

For the first time in her life, Cameron wished she, too, had a plan—something beyond getting into a sorority and enjoying college. Suddenly none of that seemed to matter as much in the grand scheme of things.

"You'd better go," Shanta said, pointing at the digital clock. "You're going to be late, right?"

"Right."

As she headed out the door and down to the first floor, she was so lost in thought she forgot she was on her way to meet Tad... until she spotted him, leaning on his car in front of the dorm. He was wearing a pair of sunglasses and his arms were folded expectantly. He straightened when he caught sight of her and met her at the foot of the walk.

"There you are!" he exclaimed. "I was getting worried. I thought maybe we got our signals crossed and you forgot I was coming up."

"I didn't. I just... I got hung up with my roommate."

"Argument?"

"No, not at all." She focused her attention on Tad, who had taken her arm and was escorting her to the passenger's side door. He was dressed very nicely in khakis and a pale blue summer shirt, with a pair of Sperry Top-Siders on his feet. His hair appeared damp and a woodsy, soapy smell clung to his skin.

"Come on, let's get going. We don't want to be late," he told her, closing her door behind her.

She put on her seat belt and when he got in on the driver's side, asked, "Why don't we want to be late? Where are we going?"

He just grinned. "You'll see."

"Where? Come on, tell me. Is this why you didn't want to park and come up? Because we have to be somewhere at a certain time?"

"Maybe."

"It is, isn't it?"

"I had to work on that landscaping job I'm doing until an hour ago. That didn't give me much time to run home, take a shower, and come back to campus."

"Where are we going? Come on, Tad. I hate secrets."

"But you like surprises, right?"

"Sure. So what's the surprise?" She looked at him, noticing the self-satisfied little smile on his lips. He had something up his sleeve, all right. "And don't say, 'If I tell you, you won't be surprised.'"

"You took the words right out of my mouth."

"Please...where are we going?"

"You sound like a broken record. You'll see."

"Well, what time does it start?"

"What time does what start?"

"You know, the thing." Cameron jabbed his arm in playful exasperation. "The thing!"

"Oh, the thing. It doesn't start at any specific time."

The idea that he might be taking her to a movie or even a concert flew out of her head. "Then why are you driving so fast?" she asked as he zipped around a corner and headed toward the highway. "What are we, like, Keanu Reeves and Sandra Bullock?"

"*What?*" He glanced at her, a blank look in his eyes.

"You know, in *Speed*. The movie? Where there was a bomb on the bus so they had to keep the speedometer—"

"Oh, yeah, that movie. I didn't see it. Anyway, we're hurrying because we don't want to miss the thing we're going to do."

"That doesn't make any sense, if it doesn't start at any specific time."

"Actually, it *does* start at a specific time, but it's always different."

"*What?*"

"You'll see."

"I can't stand the suspense! Tell me!"

Tad shook his head at her in mock disappointment. "Didn't any wise person ever tell you all things come to those who wait?"

"Probably. But I've never been very good at listening to wise people. Or at waiting."

And lately it seemed like that was all she ever did.

Wait.

Wait for the sorority bids to come in. Wait for her trunk to show up. Wait for a chance to go out with Tad again.

CAMERON: THE SORORITY

If all good things come to those who wait, Cameron thought wryly, *I'm due for some major treats.*

"Well? What do you think?"

Cameron sighed and shook her head in awe.

For a moment she couldn't find the words to tell him just what she thought.

She could only gaze in rapt appreciation at the pale turquoise waters of Biscayne Bay and the western sky smeared with pink and purple remnants of the sunset. In the distance, awash in dazzling lights, were the great pastel art deco hotels of Miami Beach.

There, Cameron knew, the legendary nightlife was just getting underway. She could imagine the throngs of beautiful people crowding the sidewalks and restaurants and clubs. She could almost hear the revelry and the throbbing Latin beat of the music that would surely permeate the air.

But the only sound out here on the water was the whipping of the sails and the gently lapping waves and the soft jazz playing on the boat's stereo system.

"Cameron?" Tad prompted, his arm tightening around her shoulder. They were sprawled on the bow of the sailboat, their legs dangling over the side, beneath the low rail. "What do you think?"

"I think this is the most incredible surprise I've ever had in my life."

He looked pleased. "I'm glad."

"How did you know to do this? To charter a boat, and drive down here...I mean, it's so perfect. Even the sunset. I just can't believe it."

"I told you we had to be here on time. I knew you'd want to see the sunset, and I figured you'd like sailing. It's sort of a 'Welcome to Florida' present."

Cameron turned toward him. She was conscious of Nate, the boat's owner, somewhere at the back of the boat, and wondered vaguely if he could see them. "It's the best present I ever got. From anyone. Thanks, Tad," she said softly and allowed Nate to slip from her mind.

"You're welcome," Tad murmured, just before their lips met.

Cameron kissed him with every ounce of pent-up passion she possessed. She opened her mouth against his and moaned as his warm tongue slid inside, probing gently as his hands tangled in her wind-whipped hair. She wanted to sink back and feel him against her, on top of her. She wanted to let his hands roam over her bare skin. She wanted to be alone with him, wanted... *him.*

"Cameron," he breathed against her ear, his breath hot and his voice ragged. "Later..."

"Yes," she agreed readily, closing her eyes and stroking his neck. "Later, you can come up to my room and—"

"What about Shanta?"

"Shant...oh, no."

CAMERON: THE SORORITY

The mood was shattered. Cameron's eyes snapped open and she looked at him in dismay. "God, I forgot all about her."

"Maybe she's not there."

"No, she's there. She's probably all tucked into bed by now. I don't suppose your family's out of town for the weekend...?"

"Are you kidding? Where would they go? Back to visit Gram and Gramps in good ol' Cuba? Or on a cruise to Europe?" He pulled back slightly, and she saw that he wore a look of disdain.

She wondered how she'd managed to strike a nerve with him so quickly.

"I just thought..." She began, but he cut her off.

"No big deal," he said with a wave of his hand, but his expression was anything but casual. "It's just that my family never goes anywhere, Cameron. My father works three jobs and my mother works two. And even then, there's no money left over for vacation. Even if there was something, it wouldn't be enough for plane fare for all of us, and my parents' station wagon is falling apart. It wouldn't make it across the state line."

Cameron nodded, wondering why she often found herself at a loss for something to say when she was with Tad. Whenever his pride surfaced—and it had a tendency to do so quickly—it was as if a steel gate slammed down between them, destroying any link they'd established.

She stared out at the water, listening to the smooth jazz coming from the back of the boat. Tad had stashed wine and crusty French bread and cheese back there, for a moonlight picnic, he'd said.

But instead of looking forward to it, Cameron wondered how much it had cost him—all of it, the boat, the food, even the gasoline to get down to Miami. She considered offering to pitch in—her father deposited spending money into her bank account every week, and she'd barely touched it so far....

But she knew what Tad would do if she asked to help pay for their date. She could imagine the insulted look that would cross his handsome features, followed closely by fury. He would take it the wrong way. And she'd never be able to explain.

Maybe she shouldn't see him again, even if he asked her. Maybe it was better to get out while she still could, before she really fell for him. After all, it could never work. Not on a deeper, long-term level. Tad had too many issues with who and what she was.

No—not even what she *was*. What she *represented*.

Or what *he* thought she represented.

"Cameron...?" His voice was soft and gentle, surprisingly so.

"Hmmm?"

"I'm sorry. I'm just—frustrated. This is driving me crazy. I've been waiting so long to see you again, spending all my time working when all I wanted to do was be with you. And now that I am, it's not enough. Now I want to be *alone* with you so badly, and I can't figure out a way."

She glanced up into his eyes, saw the way he was looking at her, and quivered. Actually *quivered*, deep in her core.

He leaned forward and kissed her, brushing his full lips provocatively against hers.

So this was what people meant when they talked about that old cliché. *Latin lovers*, she thought fuzzily, losing herself in the kiss.

Tad was impossible to resist. His temper was as fiery as his passion, but in the end, it didn't matter.

She was captivated.

The bids came in the next morning.

Cameron and a crowd of others thronged into the mail room as soon as the word spread. The air was filled with nervous, excited chatter and the sound of dozens of metal mailbox doors being flung open.

Then came the squeals.

"I got in!"

"Oh, my God, they want me!"

"Hurry, hurry, did you get one, too?"

The squeals effectively blocked out the silence that came from some of the would-be pledges as they turned away in bitter disappointment, instantly forced to envision revised futures at SFC. There would be no initiation ceremonies for them. No pledge pins. No living on Sorority Row. No loyal sisters.

Cameron's hands were actually trembling by the time she managed to shove her way to her own box, which was naturally located on the far wall of the crowded room.

She was terrified it would be empty.

It wasn't.

Inside, she saw not *one* envelope, but two.

One proclaimed her name in scrawled ballpoint pen, the other in elegant calligraphy.

One bore the Sigma crest...

The other bore the Lambda crest.

The Lambda crest!

"I got in!"

Had that shriek really come from *her*?

It had, and now she had joined the mailroom melee, jumping up and down, hugging and being hugged, congratulating and being congratulated.

Amidst all the excitement, she kept casting her eyes around, looking for the others.

Where was Val?

And Lisa?

And Bethany?

And Mary Jo?

Had any of them gotten bids?

Had Val and Lisa fulfilled their legacies and made it into the Omegas? What about Bethany? Wouldn't it be something if *she* hadn't gotten an Omega bid? Not that that was likely, but still, you never really knew.

And poor Mary Jo... what if her box had been empty?

Clutching her own envelopes tightly—the precious Lambda

one closest to her heart—Cameron set out to find the others.

And then, first chance she got, she would call all of her friends back home. She'd tell Kim and Bridget and Allison and Zara that she'd done it, she'd made it—she'd gotten into the Lambdas.

But as she headed upstairs, she realized that none of them would grasp what that meant. They'd be happy for her, sure. But only because she was happy. Not because they understood the significance of the sorority bid.

And in the midst of her light-headed elation, Cameron felt a pinprick of bittersweet realization.

Her old friends were part of another world, a world she had left behind—at least, for a while. Much as she loved and missed them, they were going to grow apart. It was inevitable.

She had this whole life, this day-to-day existence, that they knew nothing about. And they were going to get caught up in their own lives once they settled into their own schools, and she wasn't going to be a part of that, either.

Not on a daily basis.

Not the way it had once been.

But it hadn't been so long ago....

And maybe she was just being dramatic.

Maybe things wouldn't change *that* much between them.

Cameron reached the top of the stairs and caught sight of a familiar brunette head at the far end of the hallway.

"Val!" she shouted, breaking into a run, all thoughts of her Weston Bay friends sailing out of her head as she triumphantly waved her sorority bids in the air. "Hey, Val! Look!"

Chapter 10

"Has she turned up yet?" Cameron asked Val, setting her dinner tray on the table beside her friend.

Val shook her head, slid her chair over to make room, and said, "I'm really worried."

"Someone saw her getting into a cab with suitcases," Mary Jo, who was sitting across from them, said around a mouthful of lasagna.

"That's just a rumor, though," Val said quickly. "Her suitcases are still in our room. I checked under her bed."

Cameron sighed and slowly unwrapped her straw, wondering where Lisa was.

No one had seen her since she'd run out of the mailroom this morning, tears running down her ashen face.

Of course, you didn't have to be a genius to figure out what *that* meant.

"I can't believe she didn't get into the Omegas," Mary Jo said, shaking her head. "I mean, she was a legacy. Like *you*, Val. And y'all got in."

Val shrugged. "I knew that wasn't a guarantee, though. I tried to tell her..."

"We all did. But she wouldn't listen. Lisa has a one-track mind," Cameron pointed out, poking at the boring salad on her plate. No bacon bits. No cheese. No dressing. "And Val, you shouldn't feel guilty because you made it and she didn't."

"Who says I feel guilty?"

"I know you. And anyway, it's written all over your face. Get over it. Lisa will turn up, and she'll get over it. She'll be fine."

Too bad she didn't feel as confident as she sounded.

"Has anyone seen Bethany all day?" Mary Jo asked.

"No, but she got an Omega bid," Val replied. "Someone told me."

"No surprise there." Cameron speared a dry, pale iceberg lettuce leaf with her fork. "That's the last you and I will be seeing of Bethany," she told Mary Jo. "I'll bet you anything she doesn't associate with Lambdas or Sigmas."

"Who cares?" Mary Jo shrugged. "I don't think Bethany likes me very much. I heard her telling Lisa that they should start calling me Thunder Thighs."

"You *did*?" Cameron stared at her and exchanged a glance with Val.

Mary Jo smiled, but there was no mistaking the flash of pain in her eyes. "It's okay. I know my thighs are big. I probably should have gotten a salad for dinner, like y'all did, Cameron."

"No, you shouldn't have. This is totally disgusting."

"Well, I'm not *that* worried about being overweight. The Sigmas aren't all a bunch of skinny-minnies. I'll fit right in there."

Cameron and Val smiled at her, and Val said, "You're going to have a blast, Mary Jo. They have great parties."

"I know. They're having one with the Phi Kappas next weekend. I can't wait. I heard Rhett is pledging them."

"Oh, Mary Jo, are you still into Rhett?" Cameron shook her head.

"I'm totally *in love* with Rhett."

"*Why?*" Val asked. "He's a chauvinist."

"No, he isn't," Mary Jo protested. "He signed up for a Women's Studies course."

Cameron sighed. "That's just because he knew he'd be the only guy in there. He's taking aerobics, too."

"Maybe he just likes to be physically fit, did you ever think of that?"

"Mary Jo, wake up," Val said. "He just wants to see a bunch of girls bouncing around in leotards."

"Well, at least he's a red-blooded man." Mary Jo grinned. "And I'm a red-blooded woman. Pretty soon, he'll figure that out."

Cameron changed the subject. "So, Val, I don't suppose there's any chance you'll ditch the Omega bid and join the Lambdas with me?"

"Haven't you asked me that about a zillion times today, Cameron?" Val smiled and shook her head. "I'd love to. I'd *rather*—you know that. But my mother would disown me."

"If *I'd* gotten a Lambda bid, I'd join with you, Cameron," Mary Jo said. "I can't believe y'all got two bids each. But at least I got one. Hey, Cameron, why don't you join the Sigmas with me instead?"

She tried not to shake her head too emphatically. "I've had my sights on the Lambdas since I got here, Mary Jo. I really, really want to join."

"So you're definitely going to pledge?"

Cameron could tell, by the look on Val's face, what she was thinking. Val knew all about Tad and his anti-sorority attitude. She also knew Cameron had fallen for him, big-time.

"I'm definitely going to pledge," Cameron said decisively.

"What about Tad?"

"Is Tad the guy you've been seeing?" Mary Jo cut in. "Doesn't he want you to pledge the Lambdas?"

"He's just not into the whole Greek thing," Cameron said. "But that doesn't mean *I* can't be involved in it. It's not a big deal. I mean, I can definitely be a Lambda and still go out with Tad."

She just wished she were as certain about that as she sounded.

It wasn't until nearly midnight that Lisa surfaced. Val and Cameron had just returned from watching television in the lounge, and Cameron was starting to get ready for bed when Val knocked and summoned her to the room she shared with Lisa.

"Is she in there?" Cameron asked as they hurried down the hall.

"Yes, and she's a mess. I need you to help me talk some sense into her."

"What's she doing?"

"Packing," Val whispered before opening the door to her room.

Cameron spied Lisa immediately. She was standing over an open suitcase on the bed. Her back was to the door, and her long blond hair was straggly, as if she hadn't brushed it all day. Her shoulders were quaking, and Cameron realized, even before she turned around, that she was crying.

"Hey, Lisa," she said, stepping into the room, followed by Val, who shut the door. "Are you all right?"

"Do I *look* all right?" Lisa's face was puffy and streaked with mascara, her cheeks wet with tears.

"Where are you going?" Cameron stepped closer to the suitcase and saw that it was strewn with crumpled clothes.

On the floor, beside the bed, was a little pile of shredded paper. Cameron glimpsed the telltale calligraphy and realized it was a Lambda bid.

"I'm going home, that's where I'm going," Lisa said. "I have to get out of here."

"Tonight?" Val reached out and touched Lisa's arm. "Why don't you at least wait until tomorrow morning. That way you can—"

CAMERON: THE SORORITY

"I'm leaving tonight." Lisa shook Val's hand off and continued tossing things haphazardly from her dresser into the suitcase.

"But how are you going to get there?" Cameron asked. "It's the middle of the night."

"I'm going to drive. And I'm kind of in a hurry, if y'all don't *mind*." She brushed past them, sniffling, and yanked open her closet door.

"We were worried about you," Val said. "All day, when we couldn't find you—"

"Yeah, right. Y'all know you were too busy celebrating to think twice about me."

"We were not!" Cameron sat on Lisa's bed. "We looked everywhere for you. Even the library."

Lisa sniffled. "I wasn't in the library."

"No kidding. Shanta was the only one in the library. She always is." Val made a feeble attempt to smile.

Lisa didn't return it, just went back to packing.

"So where were you?" Cameron asked, because it was all she could think of to say.

"What difference does it make? Do y'all *mind*? You're in my way. Can't you just get out of here?"

"It's kind of my room, too," Val pointed out. "Remember?"

"Well, in a little while, it'll be *all* yours, so leave me alone now. Please."

Cameron said, "We just thought that if you talked about it—"

"There's *nothing* to talk about. Y'all don't get it, do you? My mother—never mind."

She was really crying now, her whole body trembling and gasping sounds coming from her throat.

Cameron was filled with pity. She wanted so badly to reach out and hug Lisa, to somehow soothe away her pain.

Lisa would probably shove her away, she thought.

Then Val did it—she grabbed Lisa and she hugged her. And she said, "I get it. I know what you're going through."

She *did* know, Cameron realized. Val, too, had a mother to whom this sorority business mattered a great deal. Val understood.

Cameron sat there on the bed, watching as Val stroked Lisa's hair and whispered reassuring words to her. And she thought about how foreign this was to her. Back home, no one she knew had a mother who desperately wanted her daughter to pledge a sorority....

Then she thought of Zara.

Was this the kind of pressure her friend was under? Did she feel this compelled to make her mother happy?

Probably, Cameron realized. She wished Zara had been home when she'd called her this morning. The next chance she got, she'd write her a nice long letter. She really would.

"I've got to go, Val," Lisa was saying, shaking her head. "I can't stick around here. It's meaningless. I'll go back home, to Bama. I was accepted. There's still time to get in. My daddy knows someone—he can pull some strings..."

CAMERON: THE SORORITY   195

"At least wait until morning," Cameron told her. "You can't go driving all that way now. It's dangerous."

"No, it isn't. I'll be fine."

"Lisa, don't be an idiot. You don't want to get yourself killed," Cameron said.

Lisa grabbed a crumpled tissue from her dresser and blew her nose. She looked at Cameron and Val, and Cameron fully expected her to tell them both to go to hell.

But she didn't.

She just sniffled and said, "All right. I'll wait until morning."

"What's the matter? You sound upset." Tad's voice sounded concerned.

Cameron carried the phone over to her bed and sat on the edge. "I am upset."

"What happened?"

"Lisa left. When Val and I got back from breakfast this morning, she was gone."

She and Val had been shocked to discover the empty room. They'd been so certain that once Lisa slept on it, she'd realize nothing was so bad she had to leave school.

But apparently, for Lisa, not getting an Omega bid was that bad.

"What do you mean, she left?" Tad was asking. "Where did she go?"

"Back to Alabama. All her stuff is gone, and so is her car.

We just got back from checking the parking lot."

"What happened?"

Cameron hesitated. She hadn't spoken to Tad at all yesterday. He'd left two messages, but she hadn't reached him—not that she'd tried all that hard. She'd been too excited over the Lambda bid, and she hadn't wanted anything to dampen that enthusiasm. Not yet.

But she couldn't put it off any longer. She'd known, just now when the phone rang, that it was going to be him. Just as she knew how he was going to react when she told him why Lisa had left campus.

"She's really upset because she didn't get a bid from the Omegas," she said hurriedly, then braced herself.

"She's so upset that she left school?" he asked, sounding shocked.

"Yeah. Her mom was an Omega, and Lisa had her heart set on getting a bid. Maybe it was more that her mom had her heart set on it."

"That's insane. I told you there was nothing good about this sorority stuff. I can't believe someone would actually throw away her chance to get an education just because—"

"Well, she did, okay, Tad?" Cameron cut in bitterly. "It really mattered to her, just like things really matter to you. Things like politics, and your Cuban heritage. This was just as important to her as those things are to you."

"It's not the same. It's—"

"Yes, it is the same. To her, it's the same. She wanted—"

CAMERON: THE SORORITY

"What about you?"

Cameron felt sick. Why did this have to happen? Why were they arguing, after such an incredible date the other night?

For a moment the thought flashed through her mind that she didn't *have* to pledge the Lambdas. If she didn't, Tad would be thrilled. If she didn't, she and Tad would have nothing left to argue about.

But that's not fair to me, she told herself angrily. *I want to join the Lambdas. I shouldn't have to sacrifice that just because he doesn't believe in sororities.*

Besides, what if this thing between her and Tad was fleeting? What if, two days from now, they broke up anyway? Then she would have lost her chance to have a great time for the next *four years.*

She didn't want to think that the bond between her and Tad could dissolve that quickly. The other night, it had felt so *real.* Like something that could grow, and last...

Well, one thing was for certain. When she told him her plans, it would be over between them. No doubt about that.

"Cameron?" His voice reached her ear. "Did you get a bid?"

"I got two."

"Oh. Congratulations."

"Gee, thanks. You sound thrilled."

"Look, I know you really wanted to get a bid, and you got two. So, I'm glad for you. If you're happy, I'm happy. Are you going to accept one of them?"

"Yup. I'm going to pledge the Lambdas."

She waited for the explosion that was sure to come.

And when it didn't, a twinge of hope darted through her.

"If that's what you want to do, then you should do it" was all Tad said.

"It's definitely what I want to do," she told him, challenging him silently even as it sunk in that he hadn't told her she was insane. He didn't even sound surprised, or angry.

"Okay," he said. "Then do it."

"I will."

There was a moment of uncomfortable silence.

Cameron was struggling for something to say when Tad broke into her thoughts.

"Does this mean you won't have time for me anymore?"

Relief washed over her. "Are you... What, are you kidding? Of course I'll have time. In fact, what are you doing tonight?"

"Working. But only till nine. Want to get together?"

"Definitely."

"I don't suppose there's any chance your roommate will be out?" Tad asked, and a thrill shot through Cameron as she realized what he was implying. And she was ready. She knew her relationship with him was no passing fling; knew that she wanted to take it to the next step. And so did he.

The thrill was closely followed by frustration, though, and she told him, "No way. Shanta will definitely be here after nine. She always is. And besides, classes start tomorrow. I bet she'll be up even brighter and earlier than usual."

Tad sighed. "We've got to figure something out, Cameron. I want to be alone with you."

"I know. I do, too. Maybe I can talk to Shanta..." She was shaking her head even as she said it, though. There was no way she could explain the situation to her roommate. Even though she and Shanta *did* have actual conversations now, Cameron could never in a million years ask Shanta to please let her have the room to herself so that she and Tad could sleep together.

"Listen," Tad said, "I've got to run. I'll come over and get you tonight."

"I'll wait out front."

He laughed. "That's okay, Cameron. I only wanted you to do it the other night because there was no time to waste."

"Well, there's no time to waste tonight, either. I can't wait to see you," she said truthfully.

And as she hung up the phone, she was smiling for the first time that morning.

Wouldn't it be totally *unbelievable if my trunk showed up today?*

Cameron had uttered those very words to Val and Mary Jo at lunch, after she finished telling them about her date with Tad.

She had been thinking that the only care she had in the world was her missing trunk, and it wasn't likely that it would arrive now. Not when everything else had worked out so neatly.

But here it was, waiting for her when she returned from the bookstore, where she'd just spent a fortune on books for all her courses.

"I don't believe it," Cameron said, staring wide-eyed at the familiar rectangular bulk in the middle of her dorm room floor. "I don't believe it."

Could life actually get any better than this?

Well, actually, it could. If Lisa hadn't left, life would be better.

Cameron hadn't realized she was actually fond of the sharp-tongued blonde until she'd seen her barren half of the room this morning. She couldn't help feeling sorry for her, and hoping maybe Lisa would change her mind and come back.

But she knew that wouldn't happen. And she knew she would never see Lisa Bettencourt again, unless life decided to throw a startling coincidence her way.

Another startling coincidence, she thought, glancing again at the trunk.

Maybe all her problems weren't behind her, after all. Now she had to figure out what to do with this thing, and all the stuff that was packed inside.

And she should do so before Shanta came back to the room. She didn't want her roommate to freak out or anything....

Not that she could imagine Shanta freaking out. Her roommate was the most even-tempered person Cameron had ever met. She perpetually spoke in the same mellow, polite tone, and nothing seemed to rattle her.

CAMERON: THE SORORITY

Good, Cameron thought. *Then she won't be thrown when she walks in and sees this giant obstacle blocking her bed.*

She started to open the trunk, then remembered her mother. She'd want to know it had arrived so that she could stop terrorizing the freight service people.

Cameron grabbed the phone and punched out her parents' number—collect.

This *was* her lucky day. The line wasn't tied up—her father didn't believe in call waiting—and her mother answered on the second ring.

As soon as Shelley Collier had accepted the charges, she said, "Cameron? Is everything all right?"

"Everything has never been better, Mom."

"You sound thrilled about something. What—oh! Your trunk arrived?"

"You got it."

"When?"

"Just now."

"Was it covered with stickers from around the world?" her mother asked dryly.

"No. No explanation as to where it's been, but I don't care. I'm just glad it's here." Cameron moved back over to the trunk and fit the key into the lock.

"Is everything inside? No one's tampered with it?"

"Let me see... Yeah, it looks pretty good. Here's my yearbook, and my quilt, and everything...."

She kept going through the contents as she continued to

talk, telling her mother about the bid from the Lambdas, and about her sailing date with Tad—an abbreviated version, of course. Her mom was pretty cool, but Cameron didn't think she'd appreciate hearing about the dilemma of having no place where she and Tad could be alone together.

"So you really like this guy, huh?"

"Definitely. We're going out again tonight."

"Just be careful when you're with him, Cameron. You're out on your own now. Be safe."

Her jaw fell open. That couldn't mean what she thought it meant... could it?

"Don't worry, Mom," she said, deciding to deliberately misinterpret the warning. "Tad's a really good driver, and he always makes me wear my seat belt."

"That's not what I mean." Her mother cleared her throat. "You don't want to go getting pregnant, Cameron... or worse."

"Mom! Geez."

"You're an adult. And I wasn't born yesterday."

"Well, Mom, you can relax. You don't have anything to worry about in that department."

Yet, Cameron added silently.

She changed the subject, asking her mother about her dad and her sisters and the weather and all sorts of boring, unembarrassing things.

Finally her mother said she had to go. "I've got to call your grandmother back, believe it or not."

Cameron's stomach lurched. "Grandma Elma?" she asked, hoping it was the right guess but sensing that it wasn't.

"No, Grandma Bainbridge. She called last night while we were out buying school supplies for your sisters. Since it isn't my birthday or a major holiday, I figure something must be up."

"Maybe she just wants to say hi." Cameron's voice sounded hollow to her own ears. What was her grandmother doing calling her mother? She *never* called her mother.

There was only one thing she could possibly want to discuss: Cameron's visit.

For a moment Cameron teetered on the verge of spilling it to her mother.

But before she could, she heard a door slam on her mother's end, and then Paige was chattering in the background.

"I should go," her mother said. "If I don't feed this girl now, she's not going to eat again. She's been on some crazy diet."

"Tell her I said hello," Cameron told her mother vaguely. "I'll talk to you again soon."

"Okay, sweetie. Take care of yourself. Love you."

"You, too."

She hung up and stood staring at the phone, wondering if she should call right back and tell her mother that she'd gone to visit Grandma Bainbridge over the weekend.

You should.

You should call right this second, before it's too late.

But her mother was going to be angry.

That's ridiculous! Why would she be angry?

Her mother couldn't possibly be angry that Cameron had gone to see her own grandmother, could she? Most people's mothers would be mad if they *didn't* visit their grandparents.

But Mom is different, Cameron thought.

And she'd definitely gotten the message, before she'd left home, that her mother didn't really want her looking up Myra Bainbridge while she was down here.

But why not? Don't I deserve to have a relationship with my own flesh and blood?

Not that Cameron planned to pursue the issue. It wasn't as if she and her grandmother had had a lot to talk about. And they sure didn't have the same interests, or the same sense of humor.

In fact, she was positive her grandmother didn't *have* a sense of humor. She hadn't smiled—not a genuine smile, anyway—the whole time Cameron had been with her.

Maybe that's why Mom doesn't want me hanging out with her, Cameron thought hopefully. *Because she knows Grandma's no fun.*

But that didn't stop her mother from making her do other things that were no fun—like getting booster shots and going through the moldy board games in the basement to see if there was anything she wanted to keep.

No, there was another reason her mother didn't try to cultivate a relationship between the Colliers and Grandma Bainbridge.

And maybe, if Cameron called her mother back right now and confessed her omission, her mother would finally tell her what was up.

Good idea. Call.

She dialed quickly, direct, and waited for it to ring.

Then she heard the sound she had been dreading.

A busy signal.

If her mother was aware of Cameron's trip to Boca Raton, she wasn't inclined to call and discuss it with her. The phone hadn't rung all afternoon, and Cameron had been too afraid to call back and find out what was up.

Instead, she had unpacked her trunk, making stacks of everything on her bed. She was standing there, surveying the clutter, when Val poked her head in.

"What the heck is all that?"

"It's just my stuff."

"The infamous trunk has arrived?"

"The infamous trunk has arrived. Help me, Val. I have no idea where to stash all this for the rest of the semester."

"What is it, exactly?"

"This," Cameron said, lifting a stuffed red plush crustacean, "is Liam the Lobster."

"*Liam*? What, is he Irish?"

"No, but my friend Bridget is, and she brought him back for me from Cape Cod a few summers ago. And this is my high school yearbook, which I've barely even seen since we just got them the day before I left to come down here."

"Why so late?"

Cameron shrugged. "I was on the staff, and I have no idea myself. I guess they didn't get to the printer's on time. This is my treasure box"—she rattled a floral fabric-covered hatbox—"filled with things I can't live without."

"Like what?"

Cameron shrugged. "I don't know. It seemed really important to bring it with me, but now I can't figure out why. I mean, I've done fine without it so far."

"So send it home. Send all of it home, along with that stack of sweaters your mother made you bring. You'll never need all that stuff."

"I know. Maybe I should send some things back. But not *everything*."

She looked again, wistfully, at the collection on her bed.

"What's this?"

"My lucky harmonica," she told Val, who raised an eyebrow.

"You play the harmonica?"

"No. But I found that on the floor at a party, and like, two seconds later, the guy I had a major crush on at the time asked me if I wanted to go out sometime."

Val laughed. "You're a nut, Cameron."

"Don't make fun of me. Whenever I carry my lucky harmonica in my pocket, things work out."

"You didn't have it in your pocket yesterday when the bids came in."

CAMERON: THE SORORITY

"You're right." She tossed it into the open, empty trunk. "That can go back home again. I guess the magic has worn off by now, anyway." She turned back to the bed and saw that Val was about to flip through a stack of framed photos.

"Hey, can I see those?" Cameron asked quickly, grabbing them out of her friend's hand.

"What's wrong?" Val looked startled.

"I just want to make sure the glass on the frames didn't break. I had them folded inside my quilt, but..." She pretended to examine the first picture carefully, though it was, of course, obvious at a glance that the glass was still intact.

The picture showed Cameron and her four best friends in their caps and gowns on graduation day last June. For once, all five of them looked good—no one had closed eyes or hair blowing across her face, the way their pictures usually turned out. That figured. Cameron's mother had taken it. Trust a pro to get the good shot.

"Can I see?" Val asked, and Cameron handed the frame to her.

"These are my friends—the ones I'm always telling you about. See if you can guess who's who," she told Val, surreptitiously stashing the other photos on the floor. In a moment, when Val had forgotten about them, she'd nudge them with her foot until they vanished under the spread.

It wasn't that she was trying to *hide* anything....

Oh, come off it, Cameron. You are so trying to hide something. You don't want Val to see the family pictures because then your secret will be out. Everyone will know that your father's black.

She hated herself. She really, truly loathed herself.

But she couldn't seem to help it. She wasn't ready to reveal her mixed background yet. Not even to Val. Not that she thought Val was a racist.

But if Val knew, it was inevitable that other people would find out. And then it would get back to the Lambdas....

And what if the Lambdas only wanted white girls to pledge?

Jesus. Listen to yourself.

Disgusted, Cameron struggled to keep up her end of the conversation with Val, pointing out her friends in the picture.

Inside, she was raging at her own shallow reasoning. If the Lambdas only wanted white girls, she didn't want to be a Lambda.

It was that simple.

No, it's not. There's no way to find out if they're racists, aside from coming right out and asking them.

And she couldn't do *that.*

No, she had to simply assume that the Lambdas wouldn't care if her father was *green.* They wanted her, and that was what mattered.

Which meant she should be able to display her family pictures on her dresser, the way Shanta had.

Yeah, and look what happened when Lisa saw Shanta's parents in the picture.

Then again, she thought, look what had happened to Lisa.

Well, Lisa wasn't the only Thayer resident who wasn't exactly clued into the old melting pot ideal. Cameron could just imagine someone like Rhett—a true good ol' boy at heart—stumbling across her family photo. He was always barging into the room, whenever Cameron forgot to close the door all the way.

She just didn't need any more aggravation. Not when everything was finally going so smoothly for a change.

No, the photos would stay under her bed—for now.

Maybe for good.

It's the only thing you can do, Cameron told herself, but that didn't stop the dull ache from building in the pit of her stomach.

Chapter 11

Cameron—Your mom called, said to call her if you get home before 11:00.

Cameron stared at the note scrawled in Shanta's distinctive backhand. It was sitting right here on her desk, where Shanta always left her messages, but she hadn't seen it last night when she'd gotten in from her date with Tad.

That, of course, was because she hadn't turned on a light.

It wasn't just because she didn't want to disturb her sleeping roommate. Mostly, it was because she didn't want to shatter the magical, dreamy mood she was in, after spending an hour making out with Tad in his car.

"Oh, man, why didn't I buy a station wagon or a van instead

of this tiny matchbox thing?" he'd asked her at one point, wearing a wry grin.

"Because you didn't know me then," Cameron answered, running a finger lightly along his strong jawline. "You know what I'm going to say if anyone asks me what kind of birth control we use?"

"What?"

"Bucket seats," she'd told him, and they'd both laughed, then made out for a while longer before she reluctantly managed to extract herself from his arms to go inside.

Back upstairs, she'd quickly undressed in the dark and climbed into bed without bothering to wash her face or brush her teeth. It had been past one A.M., and she had known she'd have a hard time getting up this morning for her first class.

Naturally, she'd overslept, then rushed around getting ready. It wasn't until just now, when she'd gone to grab her bookbag off her desk, that she'd spied the note.

She'd forgotten all about the thing with her mother and grandmother—her date with Tad had wiped it from her mind.

Now, though, the turmoil returned to churn in her empty stomach.

And even though she had less than ten minutes to get to her English Comp class way across the quad, she found herself standing still, clutching the note, her mind racing.

Her mother had called last night even though they'd already spoken once yesterday.

That meant she must have spoken to Cameron's grandmother.

Otherwise, why would she call—unless something horrible had happened to someone.

Oh, God. Please don't let it be that.

No, if it were something horrible, her mother would have told Shanta the message was urgent. And Shanta would have written that down.

Her mother had undoubtedly called because she wanted to know why Cameron had gone to visit her grandmother—or at least, why Cameron hadn't mentioned it.

I have to call her back, she thought, glancing at the phone. *Now.*

But she couldn't. Not unless she wanted to begin her college career by skipping her very first class. That wouldn't set a very good precedent.

No, she had to go. Unfortunately, she had a full schedule on Mondays—and after her last class she had a meeting over at the Lambda house. Then she was meeting Val for dinner.

The call to her mother would have to wait until tonight, Cameron thought, crumpling the message and tossing it in the general direction of the waste basket.

"Hey, Cameron! You made it, too!"

Cameron turned around at the sound of her name being called in a pronounced Texas twang, wondering who she knew here. So far, there were no familiar faces among the pledges who had gathered with her in the parlor of the Lambda house.

"Oh... hi," she said, recognizing the petite blonde who had been seated with her at the dinner a week ago. What was her name? Karen? Kelly?

"I'm Kayla Hawkins," the girl said, grinning. She slid into a folding chair beside Cameron. "Remember me?"

"Of course I remember. I'm Cameron Collier."

"Right. I figured you'd get a bid. You've got the Lambda look."

"The Lambda look?"

"Pretty, classy, not overly done up. Me, I don't have the Lambda look, but oh, well."

Cameron remembered something, then, that Val had said about Kayla Hawkins after the dinner party last week. She was a Houston debutante and her father was one of the richest oilmen in Texas. Val had met her at the Omega house and said that Kayla didn't have a chance of getting in.

"Why not, if she's so wealthy?" Cameron had asked.

"The Omegas aren't crazy about new money," Val said simply. "They're not into flashy types like Kayla, either. Which is a shame, because I like her."

Cameron liked her, too. There was something warm and genuine about the pint-sized honey-haired dynamo, despite her big, sprayed hair and heavy makeup. Today she wore sparkly, dangly earrings and a chunky gem-studded bracelet. Rings adorned most of her fingers, and her nails were ultra-long and ultra-red, with what looked like diamonds embedded in the polish. She was dressed in white from head to toe: a yoked silk shirt, leather pants, and high-heeled cowboy boots.

Before Cameron could continue her conversation with Kayla, someone rang a bell, signaling the pledges to be quiet. Ann Marie Lawrence, the sorority president, appeared and stepped into the center of the room.

"Why don't you all gather your folding chairs into a circle," she suggested, after introducing herself and the other officers. "That way we can see each other better as we go around the room and take turns introducing ourselves."

Cameron watched and listened intently as each sister and pledge stood and told a little about herself. In a matter of weeks, she thought in wonder, these women would become her sisters. She would live under the same roof with them, share meals and bathrooms and secrets with them, probably grow as attached to them as she had her old friends back home.

With a few exceptions, she acknowledged, as Randi rose and started speaking. Cameron couldn't forget what she had said at the dinner, and she instinctively knew that she would never be able to get past that.

What was Randi going to say when she found out about Cameron's background? There was no way she could keep it hidden once she had moved into the house...was there? Maybe if she didn't display her family pictures, and if her father never came down to visit—

God, what are you thinking?

She felt her stomach beginning to churn and forced herself

to calm down. She just had to stop rehashing this thing, that was all. She had to believe that everything was going to be fine.

And she sure as heck wasn't going to hide who or what she was, she reminded herself. She never had, and she wasn't going to start now.

But what if they give you a hard time when they find out? What if—

It was her turn, she realized with a start. She jumped up and spoke rapidly to conceal her nerves. "Hi, I'm Cameron Collier and I'm from Weston Bay, New York, which is the heart of the snow belt. I'm really psyched to be spending my first winter here in the sun belt, and I'm even more psyched to be pledging the Lambda Chi Kappas. I know this is going to be the best experience of my life, and I'm looking forward to getting to know all of my new sisters."

She plopped back down and saw several smiles beaming in her direction. A feeling of warmth enveloped her, and she felt her misgivings about the race issue slowly fading.

When the introductions were over, the newcomers received their pledgebooks—three-ring binders that contained vital information about the sorority, including its history, flower, secret handshake, and the words to the song. The pledges were told to study their books until they knew the data inside and out, because they would be tested prior to initiation.

Then Ann Marie went over the rules of pledging and told them to take notes.

Cameron's head was spinning when the official meeting was over.

"Wow, I had no idea there was so much to this pledgeship period, did you?" Kayla asked as they rose and made their way to the refreshment table set up in the dining room.

"Definitely not. But most of it's really no big deal, when you think about it. I mean, wearing the sorority colors on Wednesdays isn't hard—"

"Right, I have a lot of pink and gold in my closet," Kayla put in.

Cameron decided that wasn't hard to believe. She didn't have anything gold and had only one pale pink top, but she'd go shopping.

"But look at the rest of this stuff," Kayla was saying, skimming her notes. "I mean, what about this hat day thing?"

"I really don't mind wearing some crazy hat," Cameron said optimistically.

"But we have to wear it to classes...oh, I guess it's all right, as long as it doesn't crush my hair. I hate having hat-head," Kayla said. "But I can't believe we have to spend six hours a week at some runaway shelter, can you? It's so scary...aren't most runaways on drugs? Aren't they hookers?"

Cameron had to smile. "I hope not. I've never met one, personally. But I think it's great that the sorority is so into good causes."

She could hardly wait to tell Tad. She hoped he'd decide that the Lambdas had some merit after all.

CAMERON: THE SORORITY

On the other hand, maybe it would be best to avoid bringing up the sorority at all. They hadn't talked about it once last night, and they'd gotten along perfectly.

Then again, they hadn't done much talking, period.

Cameron smiled faintly at the memory of being with him in his parked car.

"What's so funny?" Kayla asked.

"Nothing..." Cameron tore her thoughts out of the gutter. "Come on, let's go mingle."

As it turned out, it was another day and a half before she managed to reach her mother, who was busy with a wedding shoot up at Niagara-on-the-Lake, according to her sister.

Finally, on Wednesday morning, Cameron heard her mother's voice answer the phone.

"Mom, it's me," she said nervously, going over to make sure the door to the hallway was closed all the way. Rhett had been known to eavesdrop outside her door, and she didn't think she wanted anyone overhearing this particular conversation.

"Cameron. Hayley said you called. I was up in Niagara—"

"I know. She told me."

"I've been wanting to talk to you ever since I spoke to Grandma the other day—"

"I figured. Mom, I'm really sorry I didn't tell you I'd gone to see her, but I didn't know what you'd say." The words escaped her in a rush.

"I don't know what to say, either," her mother said, surprising her. "I guess I just want to know why you wouldn't have told me. Did you think I'd be angry?"

"No... well, maybe. Are you?"

"No. I'm just... Cameron, you know I don't get along with my mother. And I'm not very good at forgiving people—neither is she—so I'm not very optimistic about ever having the kind of relationship with her that I have with you girls. And I hope we'll always have this kind of closeness.... I hope you'll always know that no matter what you do, I'll always love you. No matter what."

Her mother was crying. Not huge, racking sobs or anything, but her voice was tight, and Cameron could hear the emotion clogging her throat.

"Mom," she said, feeling helpless, so far away. "I know you love me. But what... what did Grandma do to you? What can't you forgive her for? I've been thinking about it so much lately, wondering what happened and why you've never wanted to talk about your parents, or see them. All I can think..."

She trailed off, and her mother said, "What, Cameron? What do you think?"

"I don't know," she said slowly, not wanting to voice the horrible thought that was trying to edge its way in.

"When your grandmother called and said that you'd been there last weekend, I almost fell over," her mother said.

"What did she say about it?"

"Just that you'd been there and that she enjoyed seeing

CAMERON: THE SORORITY

you. It was a very brief call, actually. It always is, with her."

"Well, maybe she wants to reach out to you, Mom. Maybe now that I've visited her and I'm living down here, she wants us to be a part of her life. All of us."

"I doubt that." Her mother's tone was bitter. "And even if it were true, it's too late now. We're not going to be a Hallmark family, Cameron. Not with my mother. If she thinks that after all these years, we're going to start calling and visiting each other on a regular basis, as if nothing ever happened..."

"But what? What happened, Mom? Why won't you tell me?"

"Because I don't want you to hurt, Cameron. I've been trying to protect you and your sisters from the truth. But maybe that was wrong of me. Maybe now that you're an adult, you can handle it without the kind of pain it would have caused you when you were younger."

Cameron sat down, bracing herself. "What is it, Mom? Please tell me. Please..."

Her mother took a deep breath. "Cameron, when I brought your father home to meet my parents for the first time, they threw him out of the house. Literally. My father walked over to the door, opened it, and asked your dad to leave."

"But why?" Cameron asked around a lump in her throat, picturing her proud father, wondering how anyone could ever do such a thing to him.

"Because he's black. And because my parents are racists."

So there it was.

The terrible, awful truth she had suspected all along, the truth she hadn't wanted to admit to herself.

"And when your father left, I left with him," her mother went on, her voice trembling. "I called my parents several times before we were married, begging them to accept your father, and to respect him. But they only told me to come to my senses and come home. They told me..."

"What?" Cameron wiped at the tears streaming from her eyes and fought to keep herself from sobbing aloud. She couldn't let her mother know she was crying, couldn't let her mother stop talking now that she'd finally broken her silence after all this time. "What did they tell you, Mom?"

"They told me that sooner or later, he was going to turn out to be a bum, and that I had better not dare come crawling back to them with any little black babies for them to take care of."

Cameron clapped one hand over her mouth, clutching the phone so tightly in the other that her knuckles ached.

"Oh, Mom..."

"They mellowed eventually," her mother went on, almost as if she were talking to herself. "They didn't come to the wedding, but they did send a gift a few months later. An outrageously expensive set of china. Not my grandmother's heirloom china, though... and I was supposed to get that when I was married. Grandma told me that all my life, that I would get her china on my wedding day. Mom still has it, I guess. And I got rid of the stuff she sent me. Gave it to Grandma Elma's

CAMERON: THE SORORITY

across-the-hall neighbors in Brooklyn. Mom would have loved that," she added sarcastically.

Cameron just sat there listening in disbelief.

She didn't know why she was so shocked, when she'd sensed all along that it was something like this. Maybe it was just hearing her grandmother's cruel words—

Little black babies.

She swallowed hard.

"I sent them a birth announcement when I had you," her mother was saying. "And they sent a bond. And then my mother actually called one day, when you were a few months old. She said they wanted to see you. They offered to fly the two of us down to Georgia—"

"But not Daddy?" Cameron asked, fury bubbling up inside of her.

"I wouldn't go without him. I told them that if they wanted to see you, they'd have to come to Brooklyn."

"Did they?"

"Not quite. They came to New York, just for a weekend, and they stayed at the Waldorf-Astoria. I met them for lunch. Daddy didn't come. I wouldn't put him through that, anyway."

"Did you bring me?"

"Yes. And they were glad to see you. They didn't shed tears of joy or apologize for the hideous way they'd behaved. But they were civil."

"But not to Daddy." Cameron *hated* her grandparents for the way they'd treated her father. As long as she lived, she would never forgive them. Never.

"They came around eventually, as far as Daddy was concerned. Maybe part of that is because he's a doctor now. They always wanted me to marry a doctor."

"But not a black man."

"No, not a black man. Until the day my father died, he suffered over my marriage. I know he did. He and I used to be so close. When I was growing up, I thought he was a hero. You know, I was an only child, so they spoiled me. I had everything a child could want—a huge dollhouse, two bicycles, even a pony."

"But that doesn't make up for what they did later," Cameron pointed out.

"No, it absolutely doesn't. And that's what I can't get past. If they had ever once said they were sorry for the way they'd treated Daddy—both of us, really, but he was the one they insulted, the one they didn't respect." Her mother sighed. "They never acknowledged that any of it ever happened. It was as if they'd wiped out certain memories, just erased them from their minds."

"You know, Grandma doesn't have any pictures of us on her wall at her condo, Mom," Cameron said, remembering. "All the ones you've sent her, even the family one from my graduation day—not one of them was there."

There was a pause, and then her mother said, "I'm not surprised. My mother doesn't want to have to explain anything to her friends down there. She doesn't want them to see that she has a black son-in-law and three mulatto grandchildren. She's embarrassed."

"That's disgusting."

"Isn't it? Do you see why I've tried to spare you this whole mess, Cameron? Why I can't waste any more of my life hurting over something that I can't change? I haven't forgiven and I haven't forgotten. I've just moved on. And you need to do that, too. Just get past it. Don't let it get to you."

"But how can I not—"

"There are always going to be people like my parents in the world," her mother cut in, her tone matter-of-fact now. "Cruel people who are filled with hate and intolerance, who fear anyone who isn't just like they are. You're very lucky not to have encountered more of them along the way, but you will, eventually. And you can't let those miserable people rob you of one moment's worth of happiness, Cameron. Life is too short."

"I guess."

"I mean it, Cameron. Now you know the whole story. You have to get past this. You don't have to forget it, just move on."

"I'll *never* forget it," Cameron said fiercely. She didn't know how she would ever be able to stand being in the same room with her grandmother again.

After she'd hung up the phone, she stood still for a long time, vaguely aware of the usual dorm sounds out in the hallway—radios blasting, doors slamming, people calling out to each other.

Cameron walked purposefully across the room, over to her

bed. She knelt and reached underneath, poking around until her fingers found the stack of framed photos she'd stashed there a few days earlier.

She looked at the family picture from her graduation day. There she was in her cap and gown, with her parents standing on either side of her. Her mother's pretty, young-for-her-years face smiled reassuringly at her. Her father stood there, dignified and tall, his dark eyes beaming proudly. And there were her sisters—fair-haired Hayley, who looked so much like their mother, and Paige, whose dark ringlets and chocolate-toned complexion made her the image of their father.

Tears streaked Cameron's cheeks again as she stared at her family. How could she have thought, even for a moment, that it was okay to hide the picture beneath her bed? How could she have worried about what anyone would say?

"Damn them if they dare say a word," she muttered aloud, and marched back across the room to prop the frame prominently on her dresser.

Chapter 12

If time had gone by quickly before classes started, it passed even more rapidly now. Cameron's days became a blur of lecture halls and labs, droning professors and pages and pages of notes.

Meanwhile, her nights...

Well, her nights were definitely more memorable, and a hell of a lot more fun.

She and Tad were seeing each other every chance they got—which wasn't nearly as often as Cameron would like. He was working part-time doing lawn maintenance off campus most evenings, now that he had school all day. And he spent a lot of time at the library, studying. Cameron sometimes joined him there, and they managed to go out on an actual date every so often, for frozen yogurt or even a movie.

Cameron was hardly bored when Tad was otherwise occupied, though. There was always something going on at the Lambda house, and she was getting to know most of her future sisters pretty well. She liked everyone so far—except Randi, who was usually busy with her boyfriend, anyway, so Cameron rarely had to see her.

Kayla, on the other hand, happened to be in two of Cameron's classes.

"It's like we're destined to be friends, you know?" Kayla remarked one day with a giggle. "We keep getting thrown together. It's a good thing we get along so well."

And they did. Kayla was no Val—and she certainly didn't have the potential to become as close a friend as Bridget and Kim, Allison and Zara—but Cameron liked her. She was grateful to be around someone who didn't take life too seriously.

Tad certainly didn't fit that bill. Even when he wasn't stressing over some test or debating some cause, things weren't exactly light between them.

Not that they were arguing these days. It was just that Cameron was barely able to be around him without throwing herself at him. And he certainly wasn't protesting. There was nothing like forced abstinence to keep the flames of passion raging, she thought ruefully.

Meanwhile, Val was wrapped up in her own world all of a sudden. She and Cameron still ate dinner together nearly every night, and they still hung out in each other's rooms at the dorm.

But Val had a few difficult classes, and she was busy with her Omega activities—not that she discussed it much with Cameron.

Cameron got the feeling that Val wasn't enjoying sorority life nearly as much as she was. More than once, she tried to talk Val into ditching the Omegas and pledging the Lambdas, but Val wouldn't hear of it.

"It's the Omegas or nothing, Cameron," she always said.

One rainy afternoon while Cameron was talking long-distance to Bridget, who had just arrived at her new school in Seattle, Val poked her head into the room.

"Oops, sorry," she whispered, seeing that Cameron was on the phone.

"No, it's okay, Val, come in," Cameron called. To Bridget, she said, "I've got to go—someone just popped in. Have fun, okay?"

"I'll try. But without Grant—"

"I know it's hard, Bridget. But you have to make the best of things while you're apart, you know?"

Bridget sighed. "I know. Listen, good luck with the rest of your pledge thing. Don't let them force you to do anything stupid like drink a gallon of vodka or lock you in a car trunk, okay?"

"Bridget, sororities here aren't into hazing," Cameron said with a laugh, watching Val drift into the room and sit on her bed. "Fraternities do all that stuff. But it's not allowed on this campus, anyway. So don't worry, okay?"

"Okay. I miss you, Cam. You seem so far away."

"I *am* far away. And so are you. But we'll see each other at Christmas, right?"

"That seems like a million years away. Okay, I'm letting you go now."

Cameron hung up and turned to Val, who definitely looked troubled. "What's wrong?" she asked promptly.

"What makes you think something's wrong?"

"Because you're here and not at the library or the Omega house, which is where you've been every single afternoon lately."

"*You're* here," Val pointed out.

"Because I don't have anything going on until later, when I go to the runaway shelter with Kayla."

"Oh, Kayla. How is she?"

"Fine. She's great. A little spacey, but I like her."

"Hey, what's that?" Val stood and walked toward Cameron's dresser.

Here we go, Cameron found herself thinking, realizing Val had spotted the picture of her family. So far, after all her worrying, no one had even been in her room to notice the photo, except, of course, for Shanta. And Shanta always had her nose in some law book, so she probably hadn't even seen it yet... not that she was likely to comment, anyway.

"Wow, is this your family?" Val asked, picking up the frame and examining the picture.

"Yeah..."

CAMERON: THE SORORITY

"I never knew you were part African-American."

"You didn't?" Cameron tried to act casual as she looked over Val's shoulder at the photograph.

"No, you never mentioned it. Wow, you look a lot like your dad, huh?"

"Some people think I look more like my mom. My sister Paige has his coloring and everything...."

"And this is Hayley, right?" Val had heard all about the Collier family, except for the one huge fact Cameron had omitted.

Now that it was out in the open—and Val had passed the test—Cameron felt as though some gentle, giant hand had swooped down and lifted a boulder that had been crushing her.

"Right, that's Hayley," she told Val.

"This sweet-faced little cherub actually told your old boyfriend you couldn't come to the phone because you were in the bathroom with diarrhea?"

Cameron laughed. "I forgot I told you that story. You know, it actually seems funny now. Maybe I even miss the brat a little."

"Your parents look so nice," Val said.

"Yeah, they're both really young for their ages. People are always saying that they look like they're in their thirties."

"No, I meant they look like nice people. You know, like someone you'd want to meet and talk to."

"Oh...they are nice." Cameron thought that was such an odd thing for Val to say.

"You'd never catch anyone saying that about my parents,"

Val said. "I should show you a picture of them sometime, if I even have one around. You'd say, 'Gee, Val, it's too bad you were raised by people like them.'"

"Val..." Cameron didn't know what to say. Her friend's voice was uncharacteristically acrid.

"My father isn't *nasty*," Val said, "but you can tell just by looking at him that he's not *there*. He's always somewhere else, even when he's actually home. You know what I mean? It's like his brain is a million miles away, thinking about some meeting or his next big venture—then again, I guess that's what it takes to make the kind of money he's made."

"I guess so," Cameron said feebly.

Val set the picture back on her dresser and moved restlessly to the desk. "My mother, though...she looks mean, even when she's trying to fool you and make you think that she's not. Her mouth has all these lines around it, like frown lines, and even when she smiles, it's never in her eyes. She never looks happy. Not like your parents, Cameron."

Where was all this coming from? Cameron wondered. Something was definitely up with Val. Her mood was so dark, and she never talked this much about her family, not even when Cameron asked her questions.

"What's wrong, Valerie?" Cameron asked. "Are you okay? Did you have an argument with your mother?"

"No." Val leaned against the desk and folded her arms across her chest. "Not yet."

"What does that mean?"

CAMERON: THE SORORITY

"We're definitely in for the argument of the century when I tell her what I did."

"What did you do?"

"One guess. What is the one thing my mother expects from me? Aside from being perfect in every way, that is."

Poor Val.

"Come on, Cameron, you know this one," Valerie prodded.

"She expects...I don't know, Val. What does she expect from you?"

"One hint. It starts with an o. A capital o, actually."

It dawned on Cameron instantly. "Oh, Val, you didn't drop out of pledging the Omegas."

"Yes, I did. Just now. I just called the president and told her that I've decided against joining. I was very formal and polite and she was very formal and polite and she's probably bad-mouthing me right this very moment."

"Probably." Cameron shook her head. "Why did you do it?"

"A zillion reasons. I realized it just wasn't something I wanted to go through with, Cameron. I know you're really into the Lambdas, and that's fine, but I don't want to spend the next four years of my life trying to live up to some Omega ideal. I've already spent eighteen years living up to my mother's ideal. I've done my time."

"But don't you think it would have been fun to be in a sorority?" Cameron protested. She wanted Val to live on Sorority Row with her, to share the Greek experience with her, even if it wasn't in the same group.

"No, it wouldn't have been fun for me," Val said. "I hated always having to be *on*, feeling people's eyes on me, knowing they were constantly checking to be sure I measured up. I hated spending my time with four dozen Bethany Windhams—"

"*All* the Omegas can't be like Bethany," Cameron cut in.

"Believe me, they are in the ways that count. Look, Cameron, don't try to talk me out of it, because it's too late for that. It's done. I'm out. That's it." She inhaled, then let her breath out slowly. "Now I just have to break it to the evil Eugenia Armstrong."

"Maybe she won't be as upset as you think."

"What, are you insane? Cameron, believe me, 'upset' doesn't begin to cover my mother's reaction when I tell her. You don't know how I'm dreading this phone call."

"Well, don't go pulling a Lisa on me," Cameron said, wishing there were some way she could help her friend, but knowing there wasn't.

"Don't worry. I have no intention of leaving school. I'm going to become a teacher. No matter what."

Cameron was again struck by the thought that *she* had no idea what she wanted to do with herself after college. What if she never came up with a career plan? What if she decided that she didn't want to do anything at all?

That wouldn't happen. She'd figure out sooner or later what she should become. For now, though, it was hard enough to figure out what she should do tomorrow, and the day after that.

"I guess I'd better go make the dreaded phone call," Val said with a sigh, pushing herself off the desk and heading for the door.

"Do you want me to come and hold your hand?"

"Actually, yes. But I won't put you through this. Just wish me luck."

"Good luck."

"And be ready to go out drinking tonight, because I'm going to need it."

"Fine, if you don't mind waiting until I get done at the runaway shelter. It's my first night there."

"Oh, right." Val paused in the doorway. "You know, I used to think a lot about running away when I was younger. I could've ended up like one of those kids, living on the street."

"Yeah. I guess you could've."

"I wonder if it was all that much better doing it my way, living in the golden castle under the reign of Bad Queen Eugenia," Val said, shaking her head as she left the room.

"Are you sure Val won't mind if I come along?" Kayla asked as she followed Cameron up the stairs back at Thayer.

"I'm positive," Cameron lied. She wished she hadn't spontaneously asked Kayla to come out with her and Val tonight.

But it had seemed like a good idea when they were in Kayla's sleek black Lexus, heading back to campus from the shelter downtown. And Kayla could cheer anyone up. Look at the way she'd worked magic on those poor runaways.

Cameron still couldn't shake the images from her head—all those gaunt, pale faces. You could see in their streetwise eyes that they had long since given up on finding happiness; you could hear the jaded lack of hope in their voices.

They were younger than Cameron, most of them, and they had been through so much. According to the social worker, Elizabeth, several of the kids were HIV positive; almost all had drug habits and had worked as prostitutes.

Cameron, Kayla, and two of their Lambda sisters had spent several hours with the kids. They'd brought them food—baskets of fruit, and muffins, and juice—and tried to engage them in conversations. Although one or two of the younger girls did open up a little, for the most part they were sullen and distant, clearly resenting the outsiders.

Cameron had wished she wasn't wearing a Ralph Lauren Polo shirt with her jeans, and that she'd worn sneakers instead of her leather flats that had cost more than a hundred dollars, even on sale. And there was Kayla, with her diamond-encrusted gold watch and real emeralds at her ears. At least they had left Kayla's brand-new car—a going-away gift from her daddy—in the parking ramp down the street.

"I *need* a drink after a night like that," Kayla commented as they reached the second floor of Thayer. "Those kids sure didn't make it easy to be friendly."

"They've been through hell. They probably don't feel like making small talk with people like us," Cameron pointed out as they started down the hall.

"Yeah, but at least they could be polite. I mean, I think it's just *rude* not to answer a question when a person's trying to talk to you."

Cameron smiled faintly. Kayla was clueless sometimes.

"My goodness, it's noisy in this dorm," Kayla commented, her voice raised over the volume of blasting stereos and televisions that seeped from the open doors into the hallway. "Is it always like this?"

"Pretty much."

Kayla lived off campus—something freshmen at SFC weren't allowed to do, unless they were commuting from home, as Tad did. But Kayla's daddy had found a way to get around that. It seemed he had a distant cousin living in Lauderdale who had agreed to let Kayla use her address for official purposes.

Meanwhile, Mr. Hawkins had rented Kayla a sprawling high-rise apartment right on the beach. Cameron hadn't seen it yet, but Kayla said she could look out over the Atlantic from her queen-sized waterbed.

At least, she hadn't told *that* to the runaways at the shelter.

"This is Val's room," Cameron said, stopping and knocking on the closed door. "Val? It's me."

When there was no answer, she felt queasy, wondering if Val, like Lisa, was gone forever.

Then the door opened and her friend stood there, disheveled and dressed in sweatpants. The room was dark behind her.

"Hi, Val," Kayla said in her perky way. "You ready to go out?"

"Were you asleep?" Cameron asked, seeing that Val's eyes looked puffy. Then she realized they were red-rimmed, too.

"Uh, yeah, actually I was asleep." Val yawned, but Cameron wasn't fooled. She had been sitting in the dark, brooding and crying.

"Come on, we're going out drinking," Cameron said in a no-nonsense voice. "Did you forget?"

"Actually, I did."

"Listen, Kayla and I have had a rough, depressing night and we need some cocktails. You look like you could use some yourself. So get ready."

Val sniffled. "Cameron, I don't feel—"

"Do this for me, Val. I really want you to come out. Please. We haven't gone out since classes started."

"Cameron—"

"Val, get ready. We'll wait in my room." She turned and, with Kayla in tow, headed down the hall.

"Wow, what happened to her?" Kayla asked. "She looks awful. Do you think she was crying or something?"

Duh.

"Nah, she just has allergies." Cameron wasn't about to spill Val's whole sordid tale. "This is my room. Come on in," she said, opening the door and praying that Shanta wasn't back from the library yet.

She wasn't—nothing surprising about that. Her roommate

holed up there every chance she got now that school was underway. She didn't return until midnight or later most evenings—and still, she rose at dawn to study before class.

It wasn't until Cameron was leading Kayla over the threshold that she remembered the photo of her family. There was no way Kayla wouldn't spot it—she was the type who didn't miss a trick.

Not that I'm trying to hide anything from anyone, Cameron reminded herself.

"You can have a seat," she told Kayla, gesturing toward her half of the room and walking over to her cupboard. "I'm just going to change my clothes."

"Oh, Cameron, you're not going to get all dressed up, are you?"

"No, but I've been wearing these jeans all day and I feel gross."

She wondered what Kayla was so worried about. She was the one wearing the silk blazer and pumps.

"This is such a cozy room," Kayla announced, poking around instead of sitting, as Cameron had expected. "I love that little seat and coffee table."

"Coffee table?" Cameron turned and saw that she was pointing to the second trunk, which was still sitting, lid-closed, in the middle of the floor. "Oh, thanks," she murmured.

Hmm. Coffee table. That wasn't a bad idea. Maybe if she fanned some magazines across the top, or something...

"Hey, is this you?" Kayla had picked up a framed photo from the windowsill.

Obviously, Cameron thought, but merely said yes, it was her. The photo showed her and her sisters on a Mediterranean beach the summer before.

"Who are these two little girls with you?"

"My sisters."

"Which one?"

Cameron played dumb. "Huh?"

"Which one is your sister?"

"Both."

"But not the black one!"

For the first time Cameron realized that Kayla wasn't just naive. She might not be all that bright. Somehow, that was comforting.

"Yes, the black one, too," she said patiently. "Actually, all three of us are mulatto. My dad is African-American and my mom is white. See?" Cameron marched over to the dresser, plucked the family photo from it, and handed it to Kayla.

"Wow," she said. "That's so neat. I just thought you were really tan."

"I *am* tan. I worked as a lifeguard this summer, and I've been to the beach a lot since I got here."

"No, I mean—well, like, how come your one sister is blond?"

"My mom is blond, too."

"But your sister's face is so much lighter than your littlest sister's face. And you're kind of in-between." She peered at the photo, then at Cameron.

"That's right." She decided this wasn't going as badly as she'd anticipated. With Kayla, you just kind of answered the most basic of questions.

"Huh." Kayla placed the photo back on the dresser and picked up the other one, the one that showed Cameron with her high school friends. "Now, who are they?"

As she began answering more questions—easier questions—Cameron heaved a giant sigh of relief.

"Tad, I just found out the most amazing news!" Cameron plunked her bookbag on the library table in front of him and sat down breathlessly in the chair he pulled out for her. She wasn't even supposed to meet him here for another hour, but she had practically run all the way over here from the dorm in her eagerness to tell him what she'd discovered.

"What is it?" He looked distracted—he'd been in the midst of copying something from the reference book on the table in front of him when she'd burst in.

"You'll never believe it!"

"Shhh..." Tad laid a finger across her lips. "Keep your voice down or we'll get kicked out."

"Sorry. Guess who's going home for the weekend?"

"You?"

"Me?" She blinked. "Why would that be good news?"

"I don't know...because you want to go home? You don't?" he continued, watching her face. He grinned. "Cameron, what is it? Just tell me. Who's going home for the weekend, and why would I care?"

"One more guess, Tad."

"Who—oh!"

She watched as a big grin spread slowly across his face. "Your roommate? She's going away?"

"She's going away for two whole nights. Her parents are picking her up on Friday afternoon. Some neighbor of theirs is getting married up in St. Augustine, so she's outta here until Sunday night. And you know what this means."

"Yeah, I know. Why do you think I'm smiling?"

"Too bad Friday is still four days away," Cameron said wistfully.

"No kidding. Now I'm going to be thinking about this all week, and I've got this paper due on Thursday, which I haven't even started writing yet."

"Well, get busy," she said, waving a finger at him in mock authority. "I'll just sit here and fantasize while you work."

"Don't you ever have any studying to do, Cameron?"

"Not a whole lot," she admitted, unzipping her bookbag. "But I suppose I could do my reading for psych class tomorrow."

"I suppose you could." He went back to his reference book.

Cameron pulled out her psych text and opened it to the assigned chapter. But she couldn't concentrate on reading. Her mind kept zinging from one random thought to another.

CAMERON: THE SORORITY

Initiation—it was Wednesday night. She felt a flutter of excitement at the thought. In less than forty-eight hours she would officially be a Lambda. The ceremony would be held by candlelight in the parlor of the Lambda house. First, of course, she had to take—and pass—her written test. That was tomorrow afternoon.

In fact, she'd brought her pledgebook with her, and that was what she should be studying right now, but she didn't necessarily want to push her luck with Tad. She'd have Val quiz her later, when she got back to the dorm.

Val—she hadn't been very talkative at dinner again, although she was definitely better than she had been last week, right after she'd dropped out of the Omegas. She didn't want to discuss that, although in her drunken stupor the night Cameron and Kayla had taken her out, she'd confessed that her mother had hung up on her.

Cameron couldn't imagine her own mother hanging up on her, under any circumstances. Especially long distance, when you knew you weren't going to see each other again soon.

Her mother—Cameron had spoken to her a few times, but the thing about her grandmother Bainbridge had never come up again. Whenever her father got on the phone to say hello, Cameron's heart went out to him. She couldn't shake the image of someone actually asking him to leave their house because of the color of his skin.

The family photograph—Kayla hadn't mentioned it again. Cameron figured that meant she'd probably forgotten all about it, which in turn meant she apparently didn't think Cameron's mixed-race background was all that big a deal.

Tad—if he came up to her room, he was going to see the photograph. Cameron knew he wouldn't have an issue with the news that she was half African-American, but that he probably wouldn't appreciate the fact that she'd omitted it until now. She had to tell him beforehand somehow.

Maybe she could mention it casually in passing, and then act as if she hadn't realized he didn't know....

"Cameron?"

"Yeah?" She looked up at Tad.

"What are you doing?"

"Reading?" It came out a question, and she offered Tad a smile.

"You're not reading. And you're tapping your leg on that chair. You're driving me crazy, and you're driving that guy at the carrel in the corner crazy. He keeps looking over here like he wants to lunge at you."

"Sorry." She stopped tapping. "Tad?"

He sighed and didn't look up from his notebook. He was underlining something. "Yeah?"

"Did I ever mention to you that my dad is black?"

He looked up.

He stopped underlining.

"No," he said after a moment of silence. "You never mentioned that."

"Oh. I wasn't sure if I'd told you or not...."

CAMERON: THE SORORITY

"Cameron, what's going on?"

"I just realized that I might not have told you that I'm mulatto."

"And you're worried that it's going to change something?" His eyes had grown ominously veiled.

"Tad, shhh. People are trying to study," she said, looking around.

He lowered his voice. "But why didn't you tell me?"

"I thought maybe I had—"

"No, you didn't. If you thought I knew, you would have said something about it when I told you what those Lambdas said about me that day at the sorority house."

"Oh, yeah." *Oops*, she thought.

"Why didn't you tell me? Did you think it would make a difference?"

"No, Tad, I honestly didn't think it would make a difference," she said truthfully. "I just couldn't figure out how to bring it up. I mean, I didn't want to make a big deal out of it... because it *isn't* a big deal. At least, it never has been until now."

"What do you mean?"

"I've gone my whole life without giving it much thought. I mean, sure, sometimes people looked at my family strangely, but in Weston Bay, it wasn't an issue." She rushed on, encouraged by the expression on his face. "Everyone there knew us, and no one ever talked about it or had a problem with it. Well, most people didn't. But ever since I got down here, it's like this deep dark secret or something. And I don't want it to be. Because I'm really proud of who I am."

"Are you really?" He was watching her carefully. Hopefully.

She lifted her chin. "Of course I am."

"Good," he said. "Because if you weren't, I couldn't be with you."

She nodded and forced herself to hold his gaze when she wanted to look away.

He smiled then, and she smiled back.

"Cameron," he said then, "do the Lambdas know about this?"

Her guard went up again, just as she had started to lower it. She broke eye contact. "I don't know if they know. Why?"

"Just wondering," he said with a shrug, and went back to his notebook.

Chapter 13

"**Well?** Did you study hard?" Kayla asked as she and Cameron walked over to the Lambda house after their psychology class on Tuesday afternoon.

"I hope hard enough," Cameron said. "I skipped soc this morning so that I could go over the pledgebook one more time."

"I skipped bio," Kayla said with a giggle. "I think I know everything pretty well. Except the Greek alphabet. I keep getting the letters out of order."

"Want me to quiz you?" Cameron herself had practiced that one repeatedly last night, with Val coaching her halfheartedly.

"Would you?"

"Sure, just stop me if I'm about to fall into an open manhole," Cameron said, opening her pledgebook as she continued to walk.

"But there aren't any open manholes on campus," Kayla pointed out.

Cameron wanted to sigh, but didn't. Instead, she started skimming the pages of the binder, asking Kayla random questions about the sorority, just as Val had done for her last night.

She wished Val could be more enthusiastic about the Lambdas. It seemed that once she'd quit the Omegas, she was down on sororities in general. She didn't say much about it. Still, whenever Cameron and Mary Jo were talking about pledging—something Cameron tried to avoid, but with Sigma-crazed Mary Jo, it wasn't easy—Val tended to get this tight-lipped look on her face.

Cameron knew she didn't approve of her joining the Lambdas, and she wished it didn't bother her, but it did. Just as Tad's subtle aura of disapproval bothered her.

It was ironic that the two people she cared about the most couldn't just be truly happy for her.

Make that the two people she cared about *here at school*.

The other people in her life—her parents and her old friends—knew how much the sorority meant to her. Well, maybe they couldn't relate, exactly, because they weren't down here in the middle of everything, but at least they sounded enthusiastic when she told them about the Lambdas.

Just last night, on the phone, Kim had said that she might

CAMERON: THE SORORITY

consider joining a sorority at Summervale. She'd been at school in Indiana for over a week now, and she was having a blast. In fact, it sounded like a party was going on in the background while Cameron was talking to her, and Kim was slurring a little.

Cameron hoped her friend wasn't overdoing the partying already, but didn't doubt that she was. Kim definitely had a wild streak, and it had gotten her into semiserious trouble more than once back at Weston Bay High.

"Go ahead, ask me another one, Cameron," Kayla urged, breaking into her thoughts.

"Okay, ummm..." She flipped the pages of the pledgebook, looking for something else to ask. "Did we do the sorority flower yet?"

"A pink tearose. Keep going."

"Okay..." Cameron kept flipping. "I think we've covered everything."

"Good." Kayla let out a breath as they turned the corner onto Sorority Row. "I'm so nervous, Cameron, aren't you?"

"Yeah. But don't worry. We'll do fine on the test."

"I hope so. It would be so awful to get this close and not get in."

"Don't even think about that."

"Don't you think about it, either. Because everything is going to work out fine, and Randi's going to get over it."

"What?"

"Randi..." Kayla hesitated. "Oh, I forgot. You don't know."

"*What* don't I know?" Cameron stopped walking and

slammed the pledgebook closed, hugging it against her chest.

"About Randi."

"What about her?"

"Just that when she and I were driving back from the shelter on Saturday morning—we delivered all those magazines the library donated, remember?"

"I remember. *What about Randi?*" Cameron bit the words out, bracing herself.

"The kids were psyched when we brought all the magazines in," Kayla's chatter was unnaturally high-speed, "and then, when we left, Randi made some nasty comment about how the black girls at the shelter all grabbed for the one copy of *Ebony*...."

"What kind of nasty comment?"

"I don't know, it was just nasty," Kayla said uncomfortably. "And then I said she shouldn't talk like that because one of her own sisters was black, and she said, 'What are you talking about?'"

"Oh, God."

"And I said, you know, that you were mulatto. And she said how come she didn't know that until now? She said none of the sisters knew, and that you were obviously trying to hide it. She said she wondered what else you were trying to hide, and she said they didn't want sneaky liars in their sorority."

"Oh, God." Cameron's knees felt weak.

"Don't worry. I stuck up for you and I said you were not a sneaky liar, Cameron. And then I told Mindy—you know Mindy?"

CAMERON: THE SORORITY

Cameron nodded. She knew Mindy, a quiet Lambda pledge who lived down the hall from her in Thayer.

"And Mindy said that no one else would care and everyone knows Randi's a racist. I guess Randi doesn't like Mindy, either, because she's Jewish. So then Mindy found out from someone else that Randi called this big meeting with Ann Marie and everyone and they had to vote to see if they were going to keep you as a pledge..."

"I can't believe you didn't tell me any of this," Cameron murmured. She wanted to take off running, but her feet were rooted to the sidewalk and she had to know the rest.

"I didn't tell you because I didn't want you to be upset. And I'm only telling you now because—well, I guess I slipped. I wasn't going to tell you until later, after initiation. Anyway, they voted and everyone wanted to keep you in."

"It was unanimous?"

"Not unanimous, but close."

"Oh, God," Cameron said yet again. This couldn't be happening. She felt like she was going to faint, or cry, or throw up.

Kayla checked her watch. "So listen, you're in. You don't have anything to worry about, as long as you pass this test. And we have to get there in like, two minutes, or we're going to be late. They take five points off if you're late. Come on."

Cameron didn't move.

"Come *on*, Cameron." Kayla took her by the arm, her grip surprisingly firm.

There was nothing for Cameron to do but walk the remaining distance to the Lambda house.

Nothing for her to do but take the stupid written test, which turned out to be a breeze, thanks to all the studying she had done.

She finished long before Kayla had even turned to the second page, and left even though Kayla motioned for her to wait.

She walked quickly and blindly back to Thayer, and by the time she got there, her throat ached from the strangling lump that had risen and tried to force its way up.

Only when she was back in her room with the door closed did she give herself permission to cry.

But, strangely, the tears wouldn't come.

Instead, she was filled with anger...

And a deep-seated hurt.

She was sitting on her bed, knees hugged against her chest, when Val knocked. Glancing at the clock, Cameron saw that it was dinnertime.

Sighing, she opened the door. "Hi," she said glumly. "I'm not going to the dining hall."

"Why not? Are you sick?"

"I just don't feel like eating."

"Why? What happened?"

Cameron had already decided she wasn't going to tell anyone—not Val, and not Tad—what the Lambdas had done. She planned to make her own decision about what to do....

Not that there was much question about that.

CAMERON: THE SORORITY

She couldn't pledge.

Not now. Not knowing how they felt about her—that they'd actually had to decide whether or not they wanted to keep her.

"Cameron, spill it," Val said sternly. "I can tell by the look on your face that something's up."

"I don't want to talk about it."

"Talk anyway."

And, despite her earlier resolution, she did. She spilled the whole story to Val, and when she was finished, she waited while Val sat there, mulling it over.

"What?" Cameron finally asked. "What are you thinking?"

"Well, I'm wondering why you seem so surprised and hurt, for one thing. I mean, okay, I guess I can see the hurt. But it's not as if you thought sororities were the most wonderful, open-minded, tolerant organizations in the world—"

"Why wouldn't I think that? Why wouldn't I expect to be welcome regardless of my race?" Cameron exploded. "I'm shocked that this could even happen."

"Don't be. And get used to it, if you're going to live in the real world with the rest of us. You've been really sheltered, do you know that?"

The words were unusually harsh for the normally sweet-tempered Val, and Cameron looked sharply up at her.

"I'm sorry, Cameron," Val said instantly. "It's just that I'm jealous."

"Jealous?" Stunned, Cameron stared at her. "Of *me*? God, why?"

"Because you've had this great life, and your parents are still together and your family's totally normal, and you have all these old friends you can count on, and you're at school like, two seconds before you meet this amazing guy who's crazy about you... Wake up, Cameron. You're really lucky."

Cameron frowned. "If I'm so great and wonderful, why did I almost get booted out of the sorority just because I failed to notify them that I'm part African-American?"

"Because that's the way it is," Val said with a shrug.

"But it's so lousy. I can't believe the Lambdas would do something so lousy."

"God, Cameron, if you want to join, join. But don't go around thinking that everything is going to be all pleasant and wonderful every single second in Lambda Land. It's the real world, and sometimes I think you expect too much from the real world."

"Why shouldn't I expect things to be fair?"

"Because *nothing* is fair!" Val sighed, looking exasperated. "God, Cameron, do I have to teach you *everything*?"

Cameron saw that she was smiling.

And despite her pain, she managed a little smile in return. "No, you don't have to teach me everything. Just tell me what you honestly think I should do."

"Honestly?"

Cameron nodded.

"I honestly think you should make your own decision, Cameron. Don't listen to me or anyone else. Do what you need

CAMERON: THE SORORITY

to do, for *you*. That's how I'm going to live my life from now on, and I think you should follow my lead."

Cameron sighed. "That's not what I wanted to hear. I wanted some sage advice from wise old Val."

"Sorry. All you'll get from wise old Val these days is an invitation to dinner. I hear they have lobster in the dining hall tonight."

Cameron snorted. "Yeah, right. Okay, you don't have to bribe me with lies. I'm coming to dinner with you. Just let me change my clothes."

As it turned out, Val hadn't been kidding about the lobster. Apparently, every so often, the faculty-student association splurged and treated the dorm residents to a fancy meal.

"Hey, Cameron, can I have your claws?" Rhett asked, materializing just as she was trying to figure out how to tackle the pink creature on her plate.

"No, you can't have my claws. There's hardly anything to a lobster besides the claws."

He stifled a burp. "Excuse me. Can I have the tail, then?"

"Get out of my face, Rhett," Cameron said, exchanging a weary glance with Val, who was seated across from her. "Didn't you get your own lobster?"

"Yeah, but it was, like, two inches long. I'm still hungry."

"So get more."

"Everyone only gets one. It's the stupidest rule I ever heard.

And I'm going to need my nutrition. I have to fast all day tomorrow."

"Why?"

"Hell night," Rhett said with a shrug. "It's the last night before initiation into the Kappas. The rule is, pledges can't eat after midnight tonight. That way we get totally wasted."

"That's idiotic," Val told him. "And anyway, hazing is illegal on this campus."

Rhett smirked. "Yeah, right. Hey, tomorrow might literally be Hell Night for all of us. Did y'all hear about Frank?"

Val nodded.

Cameron frowned. "Who's Frank?"

"Where have you been?" Rhett asked. "Hurricane Frank. It just trashed one of those tiny Caribbean Islands—St. Something or other. Now we're ground zero."

Cameron's jaw dropped. "A hurricane is headed here?"

"Welcome to Florida in September, babe," Rhett said, grinning. "This storm'll make one of your Buffalo blizzards seem like a light breeze."

"I doubt that," Val said. "Anyway, I caught the Weather Channel awhile ago and they said the storm had stalled. It looked like it might not be coming in this direction after all."

"I hope not," Cameron said. "I mean, it could be really serious if it hit here, right? We're so close to the ocean. What if they evacuate?"

"They better not," Rhett said. "I've been waiting too long to become a Kappa. Uh-oh. Listen, ladies, I'm outa here. You

CAMERON: THE SORORITY

know who is bearing down on us, and I don't mean Hurricane Frank."

He took off just before Mary Jo appeared. Her expectant smile faded to disappointment as she stared after Rhett. "Why did he leave, you guys?" she asked, setting her tray on the table.

"He had to be somewhere," Cameron said, wishing Rhett would at least humor poor Mary Jo. Instead, he took off running every time she came around.

Not that she'd gotten the message.

"Tomorrow's the big day, huh, Cameron?" Mary Jo asked, taking the lid off the small clear plastic container of melted butter.

"Yeah, the big day," Cameron echoed halfheartedly.

"Gee, could they have been any more stingy with this stuff?" Mary Jo asked, inspecting the butter. "I can't wait to get my pledge pin," she chattered on. "And it's going to be such fun to have a ceremony and everything. What time is the Lambda thing?"

"Seven," Cameron said briefly. "When's yours?"

"Nine. So you'll be official before me. Val, I wish you were going to join the Omegas after all."

"I don't," Val said lightly, sucking on a spindly lobster leg. "It's not for me."

"Yeah, but think of all the great parties."

"She can still go to most of them," Cameron pointed out.

"Yeah, but it's not the same. And she'll have to live in the dorms," Mary Jo went on.

"It's okay, Mary Jo," Val said dryly. "I'll muddle through somehow."

Cameron poked at her lobster. It figured that tonight was the first time in ages that she hadn't had an appetite. Tomorrow she'd be ravenous, and they'd be serving cabbage and wieners.

"Tad?"

"Yeah?"

"Never mind."

Cameron told herself it was best not to bring up what had happened with the Lambdas, even though she'd been on the verge of telling him for the past hour.

Instead, she busied her mouth by licking her frozen chocolate yogurt cone, which was melting rapidly in the steamy evening air. They were strolling along Atlantic Boulevard, hoping to catch a breeze off the ocean. The heat seemed particularly oppressive tonight, and even the gentle waves seemed subdued.

The calm before the storm, Cameron thought, looking out over the water.

"So what do you think about Frank?" Tad asked, crunching into his own cone.

"I think I was crazy to move to Florida in the middle of hurricane season," Cameron said, looking out over the water.

The sky was dark gray, but it was impossible to tell if it was just because dusk was falling, or if Hurricane Frank really was headed in their direction.

"Have you ever been in one?" she asked Tad.

"A hurricane? Are you kidding? I grew up here. They're pretty scary."

"My father called me just before I left to meet you," Cameron told him. "He was worried about me."

"Sounds like my father. He's always looking out for all of us," Tad said, popping the remainder of his cone into his mouth in one big bite.

Cameron thought of her conversation with her dad. He had warned her to go to a shelter at the first sign the storm was approaching, and told her to stay put until she was absolutely sure it was safe to go back. His voice had been edged with worry, and she hoped for his sake the storm stayed away from Lauderdale.

Then again, for her own sake, she kind of hoped it would hit, and hard.

Not that she wanted anyone to get hurt or anything.

It was just that a hurricane would mean initiation would be postponed, and that would mean she'd have a longer time to make up her mind.

Of course, she'd mostly made it up already....

She couldn't join the Lambdas.

Rather, she *shouldn't* join.

Not after what they'd done.

But somehow, she couldn't seem to entirely put aside her

original vision of her future here at SFC—the future that revolved around living on Sorority Row.

"Don't worry, Cameron, it'll be okay."

She looked up at Tad in amazement. How did he know—

"Chances are, it'll veer off course over the next few hours. The winds are shifting in the west, so it probably will head out to sea."

Oh. The hurricane.

He was talking about the hurricane.

She nodded and caught a drip of yogurt with her tongue just as it plunged from her cone.

"And anyway," Tad was saying, "even if it does hit here, you'll be all right. All you have to do is keep your head and go to the shelter."

"That's what my father said."

Tad smiled. "Maybe I'll get to meet him someday."

"Maybe you will. They're coming down for Thanksgiving."

"So that means," he stopped walking and put his arms around her, "you expect to still be hanging out with me in November, huh?"

"That's what I expect," she said, smiling.

"Are you almost done with that cone, or are you going to wait until you're completely covered in sticky melted chocolate ooze?"

She tilted her head flirtatiously. "Why do you want to know?"

"Because I really need to kiss you," he said, "and I'm not overly fond of sticky melted chocolate ooze."

"In that case..." She flung the cone into a conveniently nearby wire garbage can and closed her eyes.

Four A.M.

Cameron couldn't sleep.

In just three short hours she had to be up for her first class.

The longer she stared at the relentlessly changing digital clock and the harder she tried to fall asleep, the more elusive sleep became.

She kept going over her predicament, examining it from every angle.

In the end, there was no getting around the truth.

If she joined the Lambdas, she'd be opening herself up to the potential for a lot of pain. She'd have to deal with Randi, and with the knowledge that the Lambdas weren't as open-minded and tolerant, as a group, as she would have expected—no, hoped—they would be.

Then again, they *had* voted to keep her in.

It kept coming down to that.

They wanted her.

No matter what had happened, she couldn't deny that she was glad to know she'd passed muster with them—at least, with the majority of them.

But you shouldn't care, she told herself. *It shouldn't matter whether or not they want you. You shouldn't need to be accepted by them.*

And maybe she didn't *need* to be. She just...

She *wanted* to be accepted.

She *wanted* to belong.

Was that really so wrong? Wasn't that what *everyone* wanted, on some level, in some way?

She could just imagine what Tad would say if he knew how she was thinking.

She hadn't told him what had happened. And when he'd dropped her off at the dorm after their walk, he'd kissed her lightly and wished her luck at initiation.

If he had any idea that she was wavering on whether to go through with it...

Well, he would talk her right out of it.

Cameron sighed and rolled over onto her back, aware of Shanta's gentle breathing in the bed across the room.

The whole world is asleep, she thought grimly, *except me.*

Okay, maybe not the whole world. Maybe in Australia people weren't asleep. But everyone who mattered to Cameron was out of commission. There was no one she could call at this hour for advice; not even Kim.

Well, maybe Kim.

But Kim wasn't known for making wise decisions, anyway.

She flipped over again restlessly.

Outside, rain was falling steadily, and the wind was starting to pick up. The latest weather reports had given a fifty-fifty chance that Frank would make landfall.

Cameron wondered what would happen if the hurricane did strike.

She wondered what would happen if it didn't.

She thought about what her life would be like if she went ahead and joined the sorority.

She thought about what it would be like if she didn't.

She thought about what Val had said.

Sometimes you expect too much from the real world.

For some reason, her grandmother Bainbridge popped into her head.

Val's right, she thought, bunching her pillow with her fist.

Cameron had gone up to Boca thinking that her grandmother was miraculously going to turn into this loving person who would welcome her with open arms. She hadn't considered that the woman would be as cold and awkward as she remembered, or that her grandmother might not be capable of changing.

But that was the way things were.

Her grandmother wasn't going to change.

The Lambdas weren't going to change.

And a hurricane striking or not striking tomorrow wasn't going to change the fact that Cameron had a decision to make.

Sooner or later she had to figure out what to do.

And it might as well be sooner.

She would just lie here, awake, until she figured it out.

Oh, sure, she thought, seized by a massive yawn. *Now you're sleepy....*

• • •

When Cameron woke up the next morning, the first thing that struck her was that the sun was shining.

It streamed in the window behind her bed, bathing the room in a golden glow.

It seemed Hurricane Frank had missed them after all.

The next thing that struck Cameron, as she sat up and stretched, was that she knew...

She *knew* what to do.

It was suddenly so clear to her that she couldn't believe she hadn't realized sooner.

How could it be so simple? How could the answer have come to her in her sleep?

Maybe it hadn't—maybe sleep had cleared her mind so that she could finally collect her thoughts.

In any case, her future lay clearly before her now.

There was only one thing she could do.

And now that she'd made up her mind, it was time to get moving.

The Lambda house had never looked more inviting.

Soft, flickering candlelight glowed from the windows, and classical music spilled out into the evening air. The Florida sky was smeared pink and gold with the remnants of a glorious sunset, almost as if it had deliberately donned the sorority colors in honor of tonight.

CAMERON: THE SORORITY

Cameron paused on the sidewalk in front of the house, looking at it, and wondering if she'd made the right decision.

You did, she told herself. *You have to be true to yourself. You have to do what's right for you, just like Val said.*

She took a deep breath, held her head high, and moved up the front walk.

This was it.

Am I doing the right thing?

She hesitated only briefly this time.

Yes.

Yes, I'm definitely doing the right thing for me.

Then she was heading up the steps and in through the front door. The house was crowded and hushed, with quiet conversation and soft music filling the air.

"Cameron!" Ann Marie, the sorority president, smiled warmly from her post in the foyer, where she was greeting the pledges. "Are you ready to become a Lambda?"

Cameron felt Ann Marie's hand clasping her own, giving her fingers a reassuring squeeze.

"Yes," she told her decisively. "I'm definitely ready to become a Lambda. I've been waiting for such a long time for this."

"Good." Ann Marie smiled. "Why don't you go into the other room? We're almost ready to begin."

As Cameron moved past Ann Marie into the candlelit parlor, she told herself that very soon, this old house would be her home. She would belong here, as much a part of the sorority as any of the other sisters. She would have friends here, lots of friends.

And that was what counted.

She just couldn't cheat herself out of her dream of joining a sorority. Not now. Not when it was so close to her grasp.

Stubbornly, she thought of her father, of what he would have said if he knew how close she'd come to dropping out.

He'd tell her some story about when he was younger, back in the days when racism was more tolerated than it was now. He'd tell her how he'd managed to tear down barriers and stand up for his rights.

And maybe he'd even tell her about what her grandparents had done to him when the girl he loved had brought him home to meet her family.

Maybe he would tell her how much easier it would have been for him and her mother if they had stopped seeing each other and gone back to their separate worlds.

Easier, but not more fulfilling.

If they hadn't stayed together, they always would have wondered what would have happened if they'd followed their hearts.

They had taken a chance, her parents.

And everything had worked out.

It was Cameron's turn to take a chance, to put herself on the line and go after what she wanted.

She didn't expect the Lambdas to be perfect. Not with Randi and a few other snobs in their ranks.

But then, nothing was perfect, right?

And if this didn't work out, well, she'd be okay. She'd survive. Maybe she'd even manage to enjoy college anyway.

But if this worked out...

Smiling with anticipation, Cameron took her place by the fireplace with the other pledges.

Welcome to the real world, Cameron Collier, she thought. *It's about time you arrived.*

PENGUIN GROUP (USA) INC.
Online

Your Internet gateway to a virtual environment with hundreds of entertaining and enlightening books from Penguin Group (USA) Inc.

While you're there, get the latest buzz on the best authors and books around—

Tom Clancy, Patricia Cornwell, W.E.B. Griffin, Nora Roberts, William Gibson, Robin Cook, Brian Jacques, Catherine Coulter, Stephen King, Ken Follett, Terry McMillan, and many more!

Penguin Group (USA) Inc. Online is located at http://www.penguin.com

PENGUIN GROUP (USA) Inc. NEWS

Every month you'll get an inside look at our upcoming books and new features on our site. This is an ongoing effort to provide you with the most up-to-date information about our books and authors.

Subscribe to Penguin Group (USA) Inc. News at http://www.penguin.com/newsletters